MIKKI
AND
MEEKO 2
LOVE UNDER NEW MANAGEMENT

D51200

K SHERRIE

Acknowledgements

YOUR

NAME

GOES

HERE!

Prologue

Chapter 7: Wedding Day Blues

Santana walks into the coffee shop and spots Mikki sitting alone at the table in the back. She walks over and sits across from her best friend, looking at her as if she has eight heads growing out of her neck. Mikki continues to eat her Chicken Salad Sandwich and chips as if Santana is not even there. "What the hell are you doing Mikki?"

"I came to get me something to eat." Mikki responds nonchalantly.

"What the hell is going on with y'all? I just came from his house and he is mad as hell."

"Look, I really don't want to talk about this right now."

"Well I do." Santana moves the plate away that Mikki is focusing on to keep from having the hard conversation. "How long are you and him gonna keep playing this little game with each other Mikki?"

"I'm not playing no games. I'm really fucking done Santana. I'm done with Meeko and his bullshit."

"Who you trying to convince Mikki? Me or yourself?"

Mikki looks up at her best friend and tears are rolling down her cheeks. Her voice begins to crack as she speaks. "I'm tired Santana. I can't chase this nigga forever. I love Meeko, and I know somewhere in his heart he loves me. But he would rather watch me walk down the aisle and become another man's wife, than step up to the plate and make me his."

Santana gets up and rushes around the table and sits next to Mikki. She wraps her best friend in her embrace and begins to wipe Mikki's never ending tears. "Come on boo. You breaking and it's killing me Mik. I'm gonna take you home and...."

"NO!" Mikki says defiantly and stands up. She grabs a napkin and cleans up her face then puts it on the remainder of her sandwich. She goes in her purse and pulls out 5 dollars and lays it on the table as a tip. She finally looks over at Santana. "I'm fine. I have a wedding I need to get ready for and that's what we are gonna do. We are going to meet up with my mom and the crew at the salon, get our shit slayed and take care of whatever else is on that fucking list of hers. And then tonight, at 8 o'clock, just as planned. I am getting married."

"Mikki listen." Santana tries to reason with her again.

"I'm done talking about this Tana. I have short changed myself for far too long waiting on Meeko to do right and come around. I'm done. Starting today, what I want comes first. Now please, I really don't want to talk about or hear shit else about Meeko today, tomorrow or hell even two weeks from now. I really just want to get on with my life. And as my best friend, I need you to help me make that possible."

" Fine. Whatever you say Mik."

"Thanks." Mikki pulls her shades down over her eyes and heads for the door without another word.

Santana finally gets up and follows her outside of the coffee shop. They walk to Santana's SUV and climb in. Diamond is sitting in the backseat on her phone. She leans up and kisses Mikki on the cheek.

"Hey auntie. How you feeling?" Diamond asks with a smile

"I'm good baby girl. Your hair looks beautiful."

"Thank you. So, you all ready for that walk down the aisle?"

"Yes baby, I am." Mikki says with pride as she looks at Santana.

"Well I'm happy for you. Daddy played around too long. Time to move on." Diamond offers her opinion causing Mikki and Santana to look at each other in shock. Santana shakes her head in pity as she starts her SUV and drives off.

"Finally somebody understood me and what I was going through. I never thought it would be Meeko's 14 year old daughter that from the sound of things knew way too much about the goings on between me and her father.

After Diamond made that bold statement, she sat back in her seat and finished her conversation with her girlfriends on her phone. Me and Santana rode in silence. Only the sounds of the radio were coming from the front seat. I could tell from the look on her face that she wanted to give me a piece of her mind, and well that day wasn't over with yet, so I was also sure that she would eventually.

She really didn't want me to go through with marrying Byron.

She knew I wasn't in love with him, and my heart was still with Meeko. But like this niggas own child stated, HE PLAYED TOO

LONG. Now it was time for me to move on. I had to do what I had to do to be happy, so I was taking Diamond's advice and moving on. I had tried that before, but like the fool I was known to be for him, I allowed him and his bullshit to pull me right back. But not this time.

Meeko would NOT make a fool out of me again. Today was the day I stepped out of this teenage love and into something meant to last a lifetime. Today I was finally gonna get my Happily Ever After."

Mikki & Meeko 2:
Love Under New Management

I've Been A Fool For You
(But It's Over Now)

"We had a chance to find true love, and make it last forever.
From the first dance I knew it was just you and I, together.
What made you try those childish games? What made you want to use me?
So now today, we're not the same. And you're about to lose me.
Baby, I've been a fool for you. You gave me the run around.
I've been a fool for you. But it's over now.
It's over now."
Miles Jaye (I've Been A Fool For You)

"After the night of passion me and Santana shared with Meeko, we didn't speak for a little while. I guess once the alcohol and weed wore off, we both were a little embarrassed or afraid of what the other may be thinking. So, we gave each other some much needed space. And once we did fall back into our togetherness, we never made mention of that night again.

Everything was working out great with me and Meeko. It was like once he came home, we got backtight quick. In October we found out that I was pregnant. I put abortion on the table because although I only had one child..... that wasn't Meeko's reality and well four kids is a lot. But he wouldn't hear of it. He wanted our little bundle of joy and deep down inside I did too. I just didn't want having this baby to be an issue which is why I offered the abortion.

I worked my ass off in school from September to May and took my final exam and passed with flying colors. I now had a Real Estate Licenses that I couldn't wait to put to work. I still had another year to put in with my Business Management courses. But it was worth it because I had goals. And with a growing family, I wanted my children to see mommy succeed in her own right. Not just live off what daddy had built.

On June 12, 2003, we welcomed my little princesses Mykia Ayonna into this world. I was smitten from hello with this little girl and so was the rest of the family. Looking at her was like seeing the perfect painting of Meeko and myself. She was everything to me. My parents didn't waste any time reminding me that apples never fall far from trees so I needed to start preparing myself for her foolishness NOW. They said they were joking, but we all know its always some truth in joking. When I thought back on the shit I had taken my parents through over the years, I swear I almost left Mykia ass right there in the hospital because I already knew I wasn't gonna be able to deal.

The summer drifted on by and shit was sweet. Meeko was doing right by me and our family, even after a whole year of being home he was keeping things 100. Him and Mikey were inseparable. He made time for his daughters too, but him and his name sake were two peas in a pod. You rarely if ever saw one without the other. So, life was good UNTIL September rolled around.

The issue started when it came time for me to return to school. Mikey was in school so of course he wasn't a problem. But now I had Mykia, and I decided to put her in daycare. That's when all hell broke loose. Meeko wanted me at home, taking care of the kids and the house 24/7. He told me I needed to quit school because his daughter wasn't going in daycare. He had several fits about me not quitting when I found out I was pregnant but eventually stopped beating the dead horse when I refused to cave. Now we were standing at the foot of this bridge again and neither of us would fold on where we stood. I wanted this. I wanted this for ME. It was a part of my plans for my future and I refused to give it up. So, against everything my man said, I put Mykia in daycare and took my ass to school. The first day I walked out that door to drop Mykia off at daycare and go to class, Meeko stopped me in the driveway and reminded me that he said his peace and meant every word of it… now I was officially defying him if I dropped his daughter off at anybody's daycare and went and sat my ass up in anybody class. Before he walked away from my car, he simply told me to be sure I was ready for the can of worms I was about to open with this bullshit. Me thinking the way I think completely missed what he was really saying. I'm sitting there thinking he saying I better be able to handle all this as far as a school and taking care of the family cause he aint picking up no slack…. So my dumb ass smiled and told him I got this, I love you and we having baked ziti for dinner. With that I backed out the driveway and headed on to what was important to me, truly having no clue to the damage I had just done.

From September til February, Meeko showed his natural ass. He started being at home less and less. I naturally thought it was because of the constant arguing that had started happening between us. I reached my breaking point on Valentine's day of 2004.

The week leading up to Valentine's day, me and Meeko didn't even speak to each other. He would sleep downstairs in the den when he did come home and I of course would sleep upstairs in our bed. We rarely saw each other. When I left for school, he would be sleep and when me and the kids got home he would be gone. The day before Valentine's day, me and Santana spent the day shopping and I told her about what was going on with me and Meeko. I was really worried about us and our future together. Throw in the fact that we hadn't touched each other in over a month and this shit was all but killing me. So being the bestie she was, she offered up her babysitting services for Valentine's night so me and him could do us.

I immediately started planning a little something special for us because it was beyond time to bury the hatchet. I hadn't spent 3 whole years waiting on this man to come home just for us to be going through bullshit.

I got up early Valentine's morning and cooked breakfast, which was something I didn't usually do during the week because I would normally be running around like a chicken with my head cut off trying to get me and the kids straight for school. While Mikey ate at the kitchen table, I made a plate of Strawberry topped, heart shaped pancakes, bacon and eggs and took it into the den where Meeko was sleeping on the sofa bed. I pressed my lips against his until he finally opened his eyes."

"Good morning love of my life." Mikki greets Meeko with a smile inwardly praying that her kind words and smile is enough to melt the ice wall he has placed between the two of them.

"Good morning." Meeko responds dryly.

"I made you breakfast." Mikki sits the plate on the bed beside him and then sits next to him.

"What's this all about Mikki?" Meeko asks suspiciously.

"It's a peace offering."

"A peace offering huh? You sure aint no rat poisoning up in this?" Meeko laughs, only half joking.

"Boy please. " Mikki playfully punches his arm. "I wouldn't dare kill you on Valentine's day."

"Damn. I forgot all about today is Valentine's day." Meeko lies.

"It's cool. It's only 7:30 in the morning. You got the whole day to remember. "

"Is that right. Where the kids at?"

"Mikey eating breakfast and Mykia sleep."

"So what y'all aint going to school today?"

"They are." Mikki takes a deep breath to calm her nerves. "But I was hoping you and I could spend the day together. Santana is gonna pick them both up from school so it can just be you and I. All day, and all night."

"Well I gotta be at the club tonight."

"Oh." Mikki says flatly, feeling defeated. "I understand." She starts to get up as tears well up in her eyes. Meeko grabs her and pulls her on his lap and kisses her softly. "But you got me all day. And I promise to make the night up to you. We having a singles mixer at the club and I gotta be there to make sure shit running smoothly. You would have known all this if you wasn't fake giving me the silent treatment."

"I wasn't giving you the silent treatment Meeko."

"That's neither here nor there. So, you ready to get our day started?"

"Yes. But first I gotta take the kids to school. So while I do that, you finish up your breakfast and then we can get this Valentine's thing on the road." Mikki says with a smile a mile wide.

"Sounds like a plan to me baby." Meeko and Mikki exchange and kiss, then she hops up and floats out of the room filled with excitement about the day ahead.

"I was more than a little disappointed but was trying to make the most of it. I hated the fact that he had to be at the club tonight of all nights, but I knew this was his bread and butter and the only thing keeping him out the streets. So I put on a brave face and got on with my task

of the day so I could get down to what I really wanted. Time with the love of my life.

After Mikey finished eating I took him to school and dropped Mykia off at daycare both with their overnight bags for a fun night with "Auntie Tana". I got back home a little after 9am. Meeko was in the shower so I stripped down butt naked right at the stairs and went and joined him. I was nervous because things had been so crazy between us, but when I pulled that shower curtain back and he saw what was waiting for him an inviting smile spread across his face. I stepped into the shower and without saying a word, I grabbed the wash cloth and begin to wash him from head to toe. After the water rinsed him clean, I dropped to my knees without warning and took all of him into my mouth. That's all it took for the shower to be over and us to find ourselves in our bed with him deep inside of me making up for lost time.

It had been awhile, so I'm not gonna lie, I was thrown off when the shit passed 10 minutes. Okay I wasn't thrown off but I didn't want to ruin the day with what I was thinking in the back of my head. If I aint been fucking you, and you aint been fucking me for some time now, but the minutes you get up in it you aint filling her up damn near instantly... there's a problem. Shit I came just off him entering me, and a few more times after that…. Yet and still he was here stroking away. It was good strokes and I really just wanted shit to be right between us again so I didn't say anything. When we were finally done, we were both so spent we just fell asleep covered in each others love and wrapped in each others arms. I missed this so much. I missed it so much that I pushed what I had allowed to creep into my head to the side. I Just focused on the here and now and forgot about yesterday.

We woke up around noon, took real showers and got dressed and went on a lunch date. He took me to B. Smiths for a nice Valentine's lunch, then we rode to Chevy Chase and did some shopping on Wisconsin Avenue. He knew that would get a smile on my face.

On that cold February afternoon, I walked with my man, hand in hand, smiling, enjoying his company and feeling something I hadn't felt between us in quite some time,

LOVE.

We made it home around 7 that evening and exchanged gifts that we had split up and purchased for each other during our outing. He blessed me with a pink diamond Infinity necklace that was BEAUTIFUL. I blessed him with a royal blue Gucci shirt I came across on my search that I thought he would love, and a royal blue face Movado watch. We both were pleased, but I was so sad to know our time was about to end. It was Valentine's I was supposed to be getting ready for a night to remember with the man I loved. Not this. But despite it all I held my tears and reflected on the memories of the time we had spent together. Besides we had decided that we would get away with the kids for the upcoming weekend. Leave Friday right after school and just go. So my job was to spend this evening getting everything in order for that while he handled business at the club.

He went and took a shower and got dressed while I chilled out in the living room watching TV with my laptop on my lap looking into a quick weekend getaway that was family friendly. Vikki called and I told her how my Valentine's had just ended so to speak so she said she was coming over AND she had a surprise for me. I was cool with that because I really didn't want to be alone anyway.

Meeko emerged soon after I got off the phone and he was sharp as a fucking butcher's knife. He was dressed in black and red Gucci from head to toe. His hair was pulled back in a ponytail and he was shining bright with his diamonds. I really didn't want to see him go *and it was so hard not to cry, but I held my tears as he kissed me, told me he loved me and then hit the door. I stood in the doorway and watched him leave with tears in my eyes. Once he was gone I went inside and rolled me a blunt and broke out the big boy shit, Hennessey and Hypnotic is what I was planning to use as a comfort this night. Me and Vikki were both lonely on Valentine's Day, might as well get fucked up.*

About 9:30 just as I had completed our reservations for Great Wolf Lodge for the upcoming weekend, I heard my sister pull into the driveway. I ran to the door and snatched it open and was stuck in awe. She wasn't alone. Nikki was with her. My favorite big sister was home for a visit. I hadn't seen Nikki in a little over 2 fucking years! She was always busy with this and that out on the West Coast. She was interning at news station and she had a man so she hadn't had time to fly back home, but my baby was HOME and I was so excited to see her. After I hugged her like I hadn't seen her in a million years, because that is honestly how I felt, I ushered them inside because it was cold as shit out there.

We chilled out in the living room and began to get it in while Nikki broke the news as to why she was home all of a sudden.

SHE WAS MARRIED.

Her and her husband Darnell had eloped. They flew to Vegas, just the two of them and got married on Christmas Day. They did it this way because they didn't want it to be a big deal, and BOTH of our families would have made it just that. She was home to introduce us to our Brother-In-Law and he had a job interview here in DC. So they were here for the next 3 days. I was happy for her, although it hurt that she had gotten married without me by her side, you could see the glow of LOVE that surrounded her and that's all that mattered.

We chilled out and enjoyed each other's company and then Vikki came up with the bright idea of us going to Club Chill. The last time Nikki was in town, the club was still in development so she had never had a chance to see what me and Meeko had built together other than in pictures. But being there was totally different. So we decided to go. I informed them of the whole Valentine's bash that was going on this evening so we had to change and my closet was up for grabs. It wasn't like we hadn't worn each others clothes before.

I kept it cute and simple. A black leather long sleeved dress with a plunging V neck and black red bottom knee high boots. Vikki snagged a red leather mini skirt that was hiding in the back of my closet. I brought it, got pregnant with Mykia, hips spread a bit more, ass got thicker and all I could do was look at that skirt nowadays. But my sister put it to good use. Nikki decided on a pair of black slacks that looked as though they were painted on her. We were ready and hit the door, headed for a good time. I knew Meeko would be happy to see the girls. He loved Vikki and Nikki, even though they were gonna fuck him up that one time at band camp aka the night we found out about Santana. But years had passed and they loved him now as much as he did them. He didn't really know Amber and didn't really care for Michelle, which I wasn't surprised about at all. Shit she was my sister and as much as I loved her a lot of days, no I did NOT like her ass. But the two I had in tow, he loved so I knew we would have a great time.

We got to the club and I dropped my Escalade off with Valet and we headed inside. It was super packed and as usual, the line to get in was wrapped around the corner. I was glad I was "Mrs Club Chill" because it was freezing out there. Me and My sisters bypassed the lines and made our way into the restaurant. I told them we would work our way from the ground floor up, we would come across Meeko ass somewhere in the mix of the evening. Surprisingly, we didn't have to go very far.

We stepped through the doors just as Raheem Davaughn began crooning out the words to Guess Who live on the stage. I was stuck because I was only this man's biggest fan and couldn't believe that Meeko hadn't told me he would be blessing the stage that night. Shit I would've been here if I had known he would be in the building. I looked around and I found Meeko and the crew almost instantly. They were sitting at the largest booth in the back. This booth was one of the VIP booths/ head tables. When important people came on the scene, this is where they sat. We started making our way to the booth, and Meeko's back was too me so he never saw me coming. Him, Eric, Breon, Damien, Black Ron and Dee were all looking like they belonged on the cover of GQ this evening. They had bottles flowing, food on the table, the whole 9. Something about this shit did NOT scream business to me. It screamed all pleasure. My suspicions were confirmed when Black Ron spotted us, and I spotted his ass kicking Meeko under the table trying to warn him I was approaching. I didn't know WHAT I had just caught, but it was 100% clear I had caught something."

The girls walk up to the booth and Meeko looks as though he has seen a ghost as Mikki kisses him on the cheek. "Hey baby. What you doing here?" He asks in a stutter.

"Well damn. Nice to see you too my love." Mikki snaps sarcastically. "Look who stopped by to visit us."

Meeko stands up and hugs Vikki and then Nikki. "What's up girl? You looking good. When you get back in town?"

"I got here earlier today. You looking rather spiffy this evening yourself."

Nikki and Vikki exchange hugs and hellos with the rest of the guys as Mikki eyes Meeko trying to will whatever he is hiding in his closet to come out. Meeko throws his arm around Mikki. "It's loud as shit down here Bae, let's go up to my office so we can catch up and shit."

"Damn nigga we just got here." Vikki protest in her usual loud and ghetto manner. "Besides, yall got the bubbly and shit flowing down here. Shiiit let us get some glasses."

"That shit flat." Meeko quickly counters. "Come on I'll get us a good bottle brought upstairs."

Mikki feels his tension and slips out of his embrace and looks at him seriously. "And why you aint tell me Raheem DaVaughn was gonna be here tonight?" Mikki asks as she parks her ass in the booth where Meeko had been sitting moments earlier.

"It slipped my mind" Meeko responds with his "anger vein" in his neck throbbing.

Eric stands up from his seat. "I gotta run to the restroom. I'll be right back."

"These niggas must have thought I was green. I sat down because Meeko pretty much told on them when he started trying too damn hard to get us out of that restaurant. Then it was 12 glasses on that table and 6 of them bitches had lipstick on them. It was obvious these niggas were here on a group date. How the fuck could a super star appearing at your club slip your mind. I was ready to tear his club, the club I built with my own two fucking hands from nothing to the ground. It was hard but I held my composure because I knew it was all about to come tumbling out and wasn't shit he could do to stop it."

"Hold up Eric. Where is Alana? Why she aint here with her HUSBAND on Valentine's Day? That's odd." Mikki questions him with suspicion.
"Oh, Lil E got a cold so she stayed home with the kids. Y'all should go over there and see her now. I know she would enjoy the company."

"Yeah, I know she all bored in there by herself and shit." Damien chimes in, praying they leave immediately.

"Nah, we will see her tomorrow. We came to party tonight." Vikki states, seeing straight through the bullshit the guys are trying to toss their way.

"Let me get on to this bathroom before I piss on myself." Eric turns to walk away just as 6 women approach the table together laughing and talking. The women walk up to the table and begin to claim their seats but take notice to the elephant in the room which came in the shape of 3 women.

Only two of the women are left standing. A Kim Kardashian look alike with blonde hair and the fakest tiddies ever seen in life, and a shorter, larger Tyra Banks look a like. The Kim K stand in plants herself next to Meeko and smiles. "Did you miss me?" She asks innocently, unaware of the danger right in front of her.

Mikki stands up from the table and laughs, officially with the shits. "Yeah Meeko, did you miss her?

"Mikki listen.." Meeko attempts to try and explain.

"Mikki listen shit! Meeko I KNOW you not fucking around on me, let alone with some white bitch!"

"Michael, what's going on?" Jenna asks in confusion.

"Michael? Did this bitch really just say Michael? Y'all on a fucking government name basis?" Mikki snaps.

Meeko grabs her arm in an attempt to calm her down, as the other restaurant patrons are beginning to notice the scene. "Mikki please. Just calm down, you are making a scene." He attempts to reasons

"Fuck You!" Mikki spat as her face contorts in anger. "You tell me you gotta be here for some singles bullshit tonight, but in reality, you up in this bitch on a date? Everybody in this motherfucka on a date! You leave me at home to be up in some white bitch face with fake ass tiddies! You can't be fucking serious!

"Excuse me?" Jenna chimes in, taken aback by Mikki's outburst.

"Just shut up Jenna!" Meeko yells in fear of the situations escalating to violence.

"No! Let her say what the fuck she feel so I can clock her motherfucking ass!" Mikki looks at Jenna , daring her to speak another word. When she doesn't, she turns and looks at Eric and sticks her finger in his face. "A you, you sorry motherfucka! You fucking WIFE at home with a sick child and your bitch ass out here tryna fuck something!"

"What fucking wife Eric!" The woman he's on a date with DEMANDS to know.

"Mikki listen please." Meeko tries again to speak.

"No motherfucka YOU LISTEN! I'm so sick of you and these raggedly ass hoes. I pray on the life of BOTH of our fucking kids that she was worth it because nigga we are DONE." Mikki grabs a glass of champagne off the table and throws it in Meeko's face as he stands there looking like the ass he is. She turns her attention back to Eric. "Oh and don't think for a minute that Alana aint gonna hear about this fuck shit the moment I get to my truck. Come on y'all. Fuck these weak ass niggas." Mikki walks off towards the exit with her two sister following behind her and restaurant patrons looking on in shock.

"To this very day, I do not think there is a word in the English language that can truly capture how I felt walking out of the restaurant I BUILT for that nigga. It was like he had a fucking disease of some sort that absolutely forbid him to keep his dick in his pants. As I walked to my truck with tears in my eyes but refusing to let them fall, I decided it was beyond time for this so-called relationship to be OVER. I had to let go before I either snapped and killed Meeko, or he fucked around and gave me some shit I could not get rid of. This was no longer worth it.

I drove to DC to personally deliver the news to Alana and about her trifling ass husband. I was a friend and wanted to be there in case she needed me to console her. I knew if the shoe was on the other foot, she would do the same for me. Fuck calling someone you love like family to give them earth shattering news and then leaving them to deal with the aftermath of your words alone once you hang up. After Alana assured me she was ok, we left and I went back to Meeko's house. It didn't feel like home anymore just that fast, so I wasn't gonna call it that. But I went there and picked up some clothes for me and the kids, went and got them from Santana and went to my dad's house.

He was shocked to see us show up there at almost one in the morning, but our presence let him know there was trouble in paradise. He didn't ask any questions just helped me get my sleepy babies in the house and settled. I put the kids in Nikki's old room and I crashed in my old room. Well I didn't actually crash. I laid awake staring at the ceiling, silently crying and trying to make sense of it all. I finally drifted off to sleep about 5am but it didn't last long. I was back up by 6am just staring into space so I gave up on resting and decided to get started on my day.

I made breakfast because I needed something to do. My dad tried talking to me about whatever it was weighing on my heart but I couldn't tell him. He left me with the comfort of knowing that he loved me and if I ever changed my mind and just wanted to talk to him or needed or shoulder just to lay my head on and cry he would be there. After breakfast he left for a meeting he had at church and I just sat around the house crying in spurts and cleaning a house that was already spotless because I had to cope with this shit

Later that night, my family all met up for dinner. Nikki finally told my parents why she was home all of a sudden and they went off. They both were pissed that she "ran off" and got married. My father swore she was pregnant. That was the only reason he could see her doing what she did. I sat back and took pride in NOT being the one having them ready to lose their religion this time around.

The next day, I went to lunch with Nikki and Darnell. I liked her husband. He looked like Dwayne Martin but was taller. He had a great personality and most importantly, my sister loved him. He made her happy enough to want to spend forever with him and that alone gave him high marks in my book. While we were at lunch they invited me to come to LA to visit for a while. I was stressing how I needed a break from everything. School, my kids, my so called relationship with Meeko. It was all too much. They barely got the words out good and I was hollering hell yeah, let's leave NOW!

I went to school the following day and put in a leave of absence. I told them I had a family emergency and would be out of town for the next two weeks. When I left school, I went back to Meeko's house to pack my clothes for the trip and for my kids who would be with my mother during that time. After I packed us up, I got some cash and started loading up my truck. Meeko wasn't home and I really don't know how I felt about that. It gave me the peace to tackle the task I was there to complete BUT it also left me wondering where he was. As I was loading the last of my things into my truck, Meeko pulled up. My heart sank because I knew it was about to get ugly. We hadn't spoken in two days and now here I was moving my shit out in a sense, so I knew he was gonna have a lot to say…. And he did. Just not as I expected this time around."

Meeko steps out of his truck and smiles at Mikki loading her suitcase in the rear of her SUV. "I don't see shit funny." Mikki snaps at him.

"I do. What you doing? Running Away?"

"I'm going on vacation for a while."

"That's nice. So, who keeping the kids?"

"My mother if that's alright with you." Mikki snaps, quickly becoming irritated with him.

"That's fine. Have fun on your trip." Meeko attempts to walk away.

"So that's all the fuck you have to say to me?" Mikki snaps feeling slighted.

"Yes." Meeko looks at her quizzically. "What am I supposed to say Mikki?"

"How about fucking I'm sorry for starters!"

Meeko starts to laugh now knowing his thoughts were right. "And what is it I'm supposed to be begging your pardon for Mikki?"

"Motherfucka you cheated on me! With a fucking white bitch at that!"

First off Mikki, all you saw was me sitting in my club with my niggas. Yes, there was a bitch there but so the fuck what! What you think since we live together I can't have fucking friends? Mikki get real!"

"Oh she's your friend huh?" Mikki asks sarcastically.

"Yes. Yes she is."

"Motherfucka you don't see me with niggas all in my face hollering about they my fucking friends!"

"That's your business that you choose not to have male friends. I never asked you not to so I aint got shit to do with that."

"Fuck you Meeko! You cheated on me with that bleached blonde bitch and now you are standing here trying to fucking rationalize it! Fuck You!"

"You really need to calm down for starters. Now I'm not trying to rationalize shit. You need to grow up Mikki, it aint like we married so you can stop screaming about somebody cheated on you." Meeko explains calmly. "Next, I'm a grown ass man. I can open my mouth and talk to or sit with whoever the fuck I please. That aint gotta mean I'm fucking them. And if I was, so the fuck what! Like I said it aint like we married. You just my kids mother." Meeko states matter-of-factly.

"Wow. So that's all I am to you right?" Mikki asks in complete shock by his words as tears try to escape her eyes but she refuses to let them fall.

"Technically yes. What you think because we live together you so different from Santana and Liz? I love you Mikki, you might not believe me but I do. But the fact remains that we aint married Mikki. I can talk to whoever I please. Besides, no woman of mine would openly defy me. She would listen to her man and let him take care of her.

But that's the problem with you young ass chicks. Y'all don't understand the game baby."

Mikki slaps the shit out of Meeko's face as her anger takes over. "Fuck you Meeko! You aint shit but a fucking AIDS case waiting to happen! I swear I wish I never met your sorry fucking ass!"

Meeko smiles at her while he rubs the red spot where she slapped him. "You don't mean that Mikki. Remember, you wanted me and in a sense waited around for me while a nigga was locked up and you wasn't even my peoples."

"I wish your ass had stayed locked the fuck up!"

"Whatever. You funny as shit and being ridiculous right now. And the crazy thing is, you not even really mad about shorty at the club. You mad cause I aint running behind you right now, flipping out and shit cause your stupid ass wanna leave. BYE! Get the fuck on! Aint nobody stopping you! As long as you don't start playing with me seeing my kids…"

"Nigga fuck you! Your trifling ass will NEVER see my fucking kids again and I'ma see to that."

"Do what you gotta do Mikki." Meeko chuckles at her and starts walking backwards towards the front door of the house. "Have fun on your little trip and I will see you when you get back." Meeko uses his key to open the front door and goes inside and closes it back. Mikki slams the rear door then gets in her truck and speeds off.

"I was so beyond in my feelings. He had just carried the shit outta me. I was nothing more than his kids mother. Those words just kept playing over and over in my mind. That shit stung deep. I had his back since the day I met his

ass and this was how he felt it was ok to treat me. Now the gloves were off. I was a woman scorned for real now and I was gonna show him I was NOT to be fucked with. Meeko was so used to the Mikki who loved him endlessly. He had never met my inner bitch. Now he had just sent her ass an express ticket to come for a visit.

I stayed at my mother's house that night because I wanted to get the kids settled. I told my mother while I was gone, do NOT let Meeko foul ass anywhere near my children. I didn't want him talking to them or seeing them and I meant that shit from the bottom of my heart. That's when me and her had it out because she told me wasn't no haps. She started hollering about how ridiculous I was being and how she wasn't getting in the middle of our shit. If he called and said he was coming to get them she had no right to tell him he couldn't. I wasn't trying to hear none of that shit. To me it sounds like she was screaming #TeamMeeko, and that fucked with my sunny disposition. Sadly, I wasn't surprised. She was now fucking his uncle Slim. I was sure her newfound romance was playing a part in her unwillingness to just do what the fuck I asked concerning MY KIDS. But it was all good. I said fuck them both, I would take my babies right on out to California with me. And without another word about it, that's exactly what I did.

The next afternoon we climbed aboard our flight with my sister and her husband to leave the drama of the East Coast behind. I needed a chance to clear my head and figure some shit out about who I was and what I wanted out of this life. I loved Meeko, but our conversation in the driveway played over and over in my head. In his mind since I wasn't his wife, he owed me no loyalty. I was just his baby mother, sailing on the same ship as Santana and Liz. I wanted more than that, fuck it, I DESERVED more than that. Why couldn't he see it and why couldn't I do what the fuck I needed to do to make him see it. And what I needed to do was simple. Let his ass go.

I had decided that this two weeks I was about to spend out West was gonna be the make or break moment for Meeko and I. If he didn't see what it was like to not have me and the kids around he would never get his shit together and really step up for me… for us. So I decided to take this two weeks one day at a time, not dwell on Meeko or our situation, and when I got back home he either needed to shit, meaning come with a ring and a date and get his shit together OR GET THE FUCK OFF THE POT, and wasn't no two ways about it.

I absolutely loved that while it was cold as hell back in DC, out in LA we were funning in the sun. Mikey was truly having the time of his life. Darnell took him to a Lakers game and they had courtside seat. Kobe was something straight out of the stars in my son eyes, so having him sign his basketball made his whole little LIFE. I was also loving LA. Aside from the time I was getting to spend with my sister that I missed terribly, the shopping was CRAZY. Darnell kept teasing that we were gonna need to rent a Uhaul and drive me and all my bags back home when it was time to go. We were having so much fun that the two weeks literally flew by and the next thing I knew it was time for me and my brats to go home.

Nikki asked me during one of our late nights, chilling on the balcony, sharing a bottle of wine and putting one in the air sessions, when was I gonna stop short changing myself. I had been chasing Meeko for years and he still didn't see the value in me. According to my sister, he probably never would see the value in me because I didn't demand it of him. I accepted him and his flaws, swept his transgressions against me under the rug and constantly mended my own broken heart. I sat with tears falling from my eyes as my sister told me some real shit…. Meeko couldn't bring himself to love me because I wasn't even showing that I loved myself.

That night while the rest of the house was asleep, I sat out on the balcony alone and thought about what my sister said, and she was right. I had never demanded my respect or carried myself in a way that let him know I wasn't for his bullshit. Hell, he had his dick down my throat the very first time he got me alone in his house. I had played myself….sadly for years and nobody had said a word. I had to look like a whole fool in this man eyes. My sister had asked me to take some time, come and stay with them for awhile, until I got my head on straight. I told her I would think about it, promised her that I would. And I did. But as crazy as it sounded, I had to see if there was anything left between us.

True enough I had done all kinds of dumb shit to land and keep this man, but we had history now, a family and all. I felt like if I went home and had a real and true-blue heart to heart with Meeko, just maybe we could get somewhere and he could see me for the woman I had grown into…. Not the little girl I displayed from the day we met, up until I got on that damn plane to come here. Nothing beats a fail, but a try is something my father used to tell us as kids. So I felt like I needed to try one more time for love.

When it was time to go, Me and Nikki stood at the gate and cried so many tears. I missed my girl so much it was crazy. And while it was true we talked on the phone EVERY SINGLE DAY, sometimes MULTIPULE times per day, it wasn't the same. I was praying that Darnell got the job he came to DC to interview for because I needed my sissy back home.

I had Vikki pick me and the kids up from the Airport. She had kept my truck while I was gone, and I still hadn't spoke to my mother since she sided with Meeko. Vikki told me that he had called the house the same night we left, my mother asked him to come over. Vikki said him and my mother sat outside in his truck and talked for about two hours straight and then he left. He hadn't called anymore since then and my mother wouldn't disclose what their conversation was about. Next, she told me that she had seen him later that week at the movies, arm in arm with the same chick I had caught him with at the club. My fucking heart was shattered. I know it's dumb because it wasn't like I didn't already know what the deal was. I guess I just wanted shit to be different. Like I wanted to hear he had been going crazy without me and was just waiting on me to bring my ass home so we could make this right. Turns out that was far from what had been going down in the DMV while I was out Cali getting my suntan on and shit.

According to the Ghetto Gazzett, Alana had

gave Eric the boot. Like literally threw all his shit out in the front yard and changed the locks on him and now word on the street was that he was living our Laurel with Meeko in our townhouse. That was kinda the nail in the coffin for me. He had taken the liberty to move in one of his dog ass friends, a dog ass friend that had hurt someone close to me, so it was clear he didn't want me coming back there at all. And since he was now out on dates and shit, it aint get no clearer than that. I was willing to bet they had been running all kinds of hoes up in and out of that motherfucka. So as much as it hurt to give up on us, I had to. There was officially nothing left between he and I but our kids. I dropped Vikki off at home and went to my daddy house.

My forever home.

Over the next two weeks, I had stuck to my guns and hadn't picked up the phone and dialed Meekos digits for nothing. I took my kids to school, went to school and brought my ass on home. Some days I would go chill with Alana because she was in the same boat as me. Both of our worlds had been turned upside down by niggas we loved and it was nothing we could do about it. The first week I didn't trip, but by the end of the second week of us being back and at my dad's house I found myself feeling pissed. Meeko was being so trifling he hadn't even picked up the phone to check on our kids. That was low in my opinion and the anger I was feeling about that shit was helping to heal my heart little by little. I was slowly, but surely entering "Fuck You" mode when it came to this nigga.

Santana and I had been staying in touch of course, I mean she was my true blue best friend now. She said in the month since Valentines Day, he would cuss her out any time she mentioned me to him. I guess we both were in "Fuck it and Fuck YOU" mode. It did hurt on some level because again I had loved this motherfucka FOREVER and we had two beautiful children together, but it was what it was. I was done letting this nigga think he could do whatever because I would die without him. My name wasn't motherfucking PM Dawn.

Alana's birthday fell on the last Friday in March so she put together a girls night out shindig for a bunch of us. I was excited because I hadn't been out in a minute. Hanging out at her house gossiping while the kids played was not going out. Tonight... We Party! That shit was on her invitations and I couldn't wait. I got my dad to watch the kids for me, and truth be told he was thrilled to. I know my kids didn't come at the time or by the way my daddy wanted things to be for me, but it was no denying that since he had been allowed in their lives, he cherished every moment with them. And their spoiled asses loved themselves some Grandpa. So he kept them that night and I went out with my girls. We were at a point where we partied different. We had been going to clubs and Go-Go's and shit since fucking Junior High School, so this night we got fly and headed down to Lucky Strike bowling in Galley Place. We had reserved some lanes and food and planned to have a fantastic fucking time. We pre-gamed at Alana's house, partying to Essence, toasting to everything and having an all around good time. The damn pre-game was so much fun we damn near lost track of time and was major close to missing our reservations.

By time we got to Gallery Place, I'd be lying if I said we weren't feeling it. But we were having fun so it was all good. We parked in the garage and made our way over to Lucky strike. Our hostess took us down to our lane and everybody kinda just came to a halt. I was one of the last ones in so I didn't see what the issues was at first. Santana turned me around and was like let's just go, we can do this shit another time. All the girls were in agreement too including Alana and it was her birthday. I was feeling the drinks so I'm like these bitches tripping, not knowing what was on the other side of my girls. Alana moved to the side and that's when I saw him. Meeko, was there with the same chick. Breon,

Black Ron and Dee were there and so were three of the other bitches I saw at the club with them on Valentine's.

I stood there for a second coming to grips with two things. First Meeko wasn't shit. I don't care what nobody said, he knew we would be there that night somehow and was there to hurt me. I also knew I was truly blessed to have the group of women in my circle that I had. They wasn't ever on no phony shit. They were ready to call it a night and reschedule the whole damn shindig…. Birthday girl including just so I wouldn't have to face the pain and embarrassment this nigga was determined I was gonna feel.

On the inside, yeah I was ready to fucking explode. He was out here on dates with this bitch. Giving her his time, his attention while not even just me but OUR KIDS hadn't heard from this motherfucka in WEEKS. I wanted to break through the crowd, kick him right in his dick and whoop this trick he had on his arm oh so bad. I wanted to whoop her ass not because she was with him, but because she was with him. I know that sound crazy as hell but listen. When I ran up on this bitch with him at the club, I went in on HIM. The nigga I had a relationship with. I dismissed her in so many words. Yeah I threatened to knock her shit loose BUT that was only after she said something directed towards me. Once she heeded my warning and shut her fucking pie hole I left her alone. BUT NOW things were different. This bitch found out weeks ago that this nigga had a family at home. By default she was supposed to step the fuck off... doesn't matter if I stayed with his ass or left, she was supposed to remove herself from this situation. She chose not to do that. Now here we are weeks later and I gotta look at this plastic bitch on his arm while me and my friends were out TRYING to have a god damn time. I was LIVID on the inside. I was also crushed. But let me tell you something..... pride is a motherfucka.

Breon had already spotted us. Knowing that he saw us, I refused to leave. Why did I have to be the one at home crying and shit, feeling bad about what had gone down while this nigga get to live life and keep smiling. I refused to let them see me sweat. If he was cool with the split, then damnit so was I. So I assured my girls I was fine and we continued on to our lanes.... That was a section down from their's and got the party started.

We ate good, we drank even better and had a fucking blast. I thought it was gonna be hard for me not to acknowledge what was going on down the aisle from me but once we got into the swing of things it wasn't hard at all. Alana had been like another sister to me since I first met her back in the day so I wasn't gonna ruin her birthday with my bullshit. I would deal with my broken heart later.

I don't even know what time Meeko and his crew left, but we shut the fucking bowling alley down. By time we left I was damn near on my head. I threw up in the middle of 7ᵗʰ street as we all tried to hold each other up and make it to the parking garage…. Knowing damn well we aint have no business driving nothing. I rode with Alana since we lived blocks from each other so I climbed in the backseat and her and Vikki got in the front and the damn finally gave way and I cried until my drunk ass fell asleep while her and Vikki was talking about how surprised they were that I didn't kill the bitch Meeko had with him. I had displayed so much growth that night. They had no clue how hard that shit was. I laid back there and cried, not a boohooing snot filled cry but a silent cry. But what nobody on the outside looking in knew was that I was crying because it was clear to me that things were officially over between Meeko and I.

I woke up the next afternoon about 2pm on Alana's sofa. I was fucked up the night before so I wasn't about to even go in my daddy house. I grabbed my phone to call my dad and check on my kids and I saw I had 21 missed calls from Meeko. The first one came at 3am and I had just missed one 10 minutes before I woke up. Inside I was worried, because we hadn't spoke in a minute so what the fuck was he calling me for now. I sat up and grabbed one of Alana's jacks of the coffee table and sparked it then called him back. Surprisingly he answered on the first ring as if he had been waiting on me or something."

"Hello." Meeko answers

"Hey you called me?"

"Yeah. What you just getting up?"

"Yeah. Why?" Mikki asks, looking at the phone with the stank face.

"Cause I've been calling your ass all morning Mikki. That's why."

"Why you just aint leave a message?"

"Damn, that's how you feel about me now? Just leave a message huh?"

"Meeko don't start. What do you want?"

"I wanted to know if it was alright if I come and pick up the kids today."

"When you keeping them until?"

"Tomorrow night if that's cool with you."

"That's fine by me. What time are you coming to get them?"

"Give me about an hour or so."

"Cool." Mikki hangs up the phone, not having anything else to say about the situation.

"I knew Meeko well enough to know that an hour for him really meant like 3 hours, so I had some time to go get the kids right. I went in

Alana's room and me and her put one in the air and talked about what had gone down last night. It was crazy how good this nigga looked, but seeing him with that bitch on his arm did something to my spirit. That shit hurt. She was telling me how hard it was for her last night NOT seeing Eric ass there. Because all night her mind wandered, worried about where he may have been and who he may have been with. Me and Alana were one in the same. We put on a good front in front of the world like we were unbothered by our relationships crashing but with each other we were vulnerable and that helped us to help each other make it through this fluke shit. Since her kids were gone for the weekend and mine were about to go we decided we were gonna go out to the movies that night.

I left and went to my father's house to get the kids together. I didn't mention to Mikey that Meeko was coming to get them because I really didn't know if he was gonna show up. Shit it had been over a month since he had even dialed a number to speak to our children, so I really didn't know what kind of shit he was on and I wasn't gonna open my baby up to that kind of hurt. Meeko would have saw a side of me he had never seen before. You could fuck over me, lie to me, cheat on me... whatever. I was grown and would get over the shit eventually, but my BABIES... NAH. Hurting them was a quick way to get fucked up.

Finally at almost 7pm that evening, Mikey was on the porch with his little friends and came FLYING through the house like a bat out of hell screaming that his daddy was outside. By this time, I was dressed and ready to roll since me and Alana had plans. I was just waiting on him to come and get them. I grabbed Mykia and her diaper bag and followed Mikey back outside. It was crazy how just the sight of Meeko foul ass had my child beaming like a kid on Christmas morning."

Meeko hops out his truck and walks to the gate as Mikki comes down the stairs carrying Mykia. She hands her and the diaper bag over to him. He gives Mikki a once over from head to toe and smiles. "You look nice."

"I always look nice." Mikki responds matter-of-factly.

"You going out?"

"Why?" Mikki snaps with an attitude.

"I was just asking Mikki. No need for the hostility."

"Daddy, are we going with you?" Mikey asks unable to hold back his excitement.

"Yeah big man. Y'all kicking it with daddy tonight."

Mikey looks you at Mikki with pleading eyes. "You coming too mommy?"

Mikki stoops down and kisses Mikey on the cheek. "No baby. You and your sister are gonna spend some time with your father and I'll see you tomorrow."

"You coming home tomorrow?" Mikey asks with

even more excitement.

"No baby. You and your sister are coming back here. Remember we talked about all of this Mikey." Meeko looks at Mikki sincerely and grabs her hand. "You know you could come home if you want to Mikki."

"Thanks, but no thanks." Mikki responds with a smile. She leans in and kisses Mykia on her forehead and then kisses Mikey on his cheek again. "I love yall and will see yall tomorrow okay. And Mikey, you take care of your sister."

"I will mommy. I always take care of the brat." Mikey jokes as he tickles Mykia causing her to crack up laughing.

"Alright, I will see y'all later." Mikki finally opens the gate and Meeko steps to the side so she could walk out. She walks passed him and heads for her truck.

"Aye Mikki, hold up. Let me holla at you right quick."

"Can it wait?" Mikki responds in an annoyed tone.

"Nah, it can't."

"Well I will call you later cause I'm running late for my date."

"Your date?" Meeko asks, eyeing Mikki with confusion.

"That's what I said." Mikki blushes as she climbs in her truck and closes the door without another word.

Meeko rushes to his truck and puts Mykia in her carseat in the back while Mikey climbs up in the front passenger seat. He walks over to the driver's side of Mikki's truck and taps on her window. She hangs up her phone and puts it down then rolls down her window. "It's really not wise of you to leave them in a running vehicle Meeko."

"They fine. But fuck all that. What's this about you going on a date? What was that a joke or some shit?"

"Not at all Meeko.

"So you dating now Mikki?" He asks in disbelief.

"Nigga aren't you?"

"Fuck no." Meeko lies.

"Well that's too bad boo. You might want to start then."

"So who the fuck is he?"

"Oh don't worry, it aint nobody you know or no shit like that. Now excuse me, I'm already running late and you making me later."

"Aye Mikki for the last time stop fucking playing with me."

"Meeko aint nobody playing with your ass. You had me. You had me right in the palm of your hands and YOU fucked that up. Now I'm not wasting another second on this tired ass shit. Now MOVE."

Meeko looks at her with both shock and hurt covering his face. "Damn Mikki, so it's like that?"

"Nigga you made it this way. Now bye."

"Alright. You got that." Meeko throws his hands up in mock surrender then backs across the street to his truck. Mikki pulls out of her parking space and drives off leaving him right where he stood.

"Now you and I both know I wasn't going on no date. But his ass didn't need to know that. It was nice to see him sweat. To see him feel the shit he constantly made me feel. It was beyond time for Meeko to know that the sun didn't rise and set out his ass.

I drove down to Alana's house and picked her up and we headed out to VA and went to Red

Lobster to get our night started with some seafood and some drinks. After dinner we went and got our movie tickets but still had like an hour to kill so we sat in the parking lot and put one in the air. By the time we were headed into Springfield Mall for the movie we were nice, and having a laugh of the night at the donkey of the day. Meeko was blowing my shit up, calling me back to back to back like a fucking callbot. I guess he thought this would ruin the date I was supposedly on. I let him get his game on for about an hour while we were in the parking lot blazing, but when we got ready to go in the movie, I shut his shit down by simply powering my phone off. I knew he was probably ready to bust a fucking blood vessel when that bitch started going straight to voicemail. About 5 minutes after I turned my shit off, Alana shit started blowing up. She told me she had talked to Eric earlier and told him we were going to the movies, so I know this nigga probably thought we were on a double date now. Alana quickly powering her shit off didn't make it any better.

Now the funny thing is, when we left home we had no intentions of being on no double date. This was just us getting out the house. However, as we were walking to the movie theater we came across a set of familiar faces.

Back in the day before he went in and Eric

stole her away, Alana used to fuck with this dude Gabby that was also from Trinidad. Alana used to always say if he hadn't went in, all her kids would've had this nigga last name. Don't get it twisted, she loved Eric, but it was no denying that Gabby made her heart skip a beat or two back in the day. And the nigga standing beside him made a bitch do a double take. His name was Chico and this nigga was FIONE. He was about 5'10, red bone, nice goat tee and mustache, tats galore and had a little cut to him that showed he made it to the gym a few times a month or so. It wasn't nothing major. But I had known him since we first moved on the scene back in the day but oddly enough I never saw Chico in that light. His sexy had never managed to shine through, I guess because since I was 12 years old I was blind to every nigga walking except Meeko stupid ass.

Gabby came over to speak to Alana because it had been some time since they had seen each other. Word on the street was he was home but he hadn't been on the scene for whatever reason, so they hadn't seen each other in forever. They hugged up like they had never stopped fucking with each other and I swear if I didn't know my girl the way I did, I would've been side-eyeing the shit out of her the way she fell into this nigga embrace…. Like it was all the fuck she needed to survive or some shit.

It turned out that they were heading in to see the same movie as we were, so we decided to sit together. It wasn't spoken, it just happened. Through the whole movie, Gabby and Alanaa were having maaaaad conversation. Okay it was more like he was doing maaad whispering in her ear and her ass was doing maaaaad school girl giggling. I hadn't seen her ass this Giddy in a minute. Not even the last few months of her and Eric's relationship had I witnessed this much showing of the full set of 32. This bitch was on ONE!

Chico and I spoke, but aside from that it was nothing. He offered me some of his popcorn and I declined. I was seriously focused on fucking up my peanut M&M's and my cherry Pepsi, while making notes on what to cuss Alana ass out about the minute we got out this bitch. The movie ended up being dumb as shit, so we decided to break out in the middle of it. Once we got outside, Gabby and Chico invited us to come and grab some dinner with them. True enough we had already eaten before we came to the movies but Alana had fucking hearts dancing in her eyes, having a ball with her lost one, I didn't want to shit on her night so I agreed to tag along.

We headed right back to the same Red Lobster Alana and I had ate at a few hours earlier. Me and her ordered drinks and enjoyed the conversation while they grubbed. When we left there, Gabby and Alana wanted to go to the park to chill. Since I was her ride and Chico was his, we automatically got dragged into the mix. So without complaint we headed down Anacostia park off the late night. Gabby and Alana went off walking hand in hand to talk and shit and left me and Chico sitting on a picnic bench.

It was awkward as hell at first. Neither of us really had too much to say to the other. It was like if it wasn't for our friends we wouldn't even the fuck be there so nah, we wasn't bursting with shit to talk about off the break. I also believe him knowing that I was Meeko's kids mother played a huge part in how he handled me. Everybody knew that nigga and I guess he aint want to say nothing that could be misconstrued. I also knew his baby mother Kendra. We weren't friends or no shit like that but everybody in Trinidad knew everybody in Trinidad. That was just how shit was. Even if you aint fuck with them, you knew them and that was the case with me and Kendra. We aint rock, but we knew each other.

Finally, after about 45 minutes of pregnant pauses and closed ended questions, Chico brought up the day me and my sisters wrecked Breon baby mother and her folks right outside our house back in the day. That conversation got us to laughing and talking and then shit just started to flow. We talked about some of the crazy shit we had witnessed back in the day, fights, hook ups and all kinds of shit. We even spilled a bit about what it was like for me being a PK on the block. It felt like as soon as we started really kicking it, it started to rain. Gabby invited us back to his place, but Alana and I both agreed that would be a inappropriate. We didn't say shit to them about it but we both were a little buzzed and lets keep it real…. Shit happens. So we passed on the Electric Relaxation and decided to call it a night. As me and Alana climbed up in my truck, Chico shot me a wink that caused me to blush like a school girl. It happened so fast that I didn't think Alana ass saw it, but a bitch was so wrong and her ass clowned me all the way the fuck home.

I dropped her off and then I headed on in the house and crashed. It was almost 2am and I knew I had to get up soon because while my daddy had welcomed me and my babies home with opened arms, he also reminded me that the rules in his house was still the same. Sunday was the Lords day and if you rested your head under HIS roof, come Sunday morning that ass would be in a pew. So at 7am, despite my slight hangover and how tired I was, my ass was up getting ready for church. My dad preached a good sermon as always, but in the back of my mind I couldn't wait for service to end so I could break out. Again, I was tired. I stuck around for breakfast because my dad asked me to. I chatted with Michelle and her creepy ass husband Will during fellowship breakfast. I really was not a fan of Will and always tried to keep my interactions with his ass to a minimum. He was so fucking smug and fake holier than thou and I couldn't stand his ass. Throw in the times I caught him openly checking me out. He was a snake but for whatever reason, my sister loved his fake fly ass and Pastor Ike fucking ADORDED this nigga. Like seriously he would talk about this creep ass nigga like he was something sent directly from God. My mother used to say she think my father fucked with Will so tough because he always wanted a son but ended up with five daughters. Will was his first son-in-law so that made him the holy grail. But Malissa aint fuck with him too tough either. She said she got the same snake in the grass vibe from his ass so we played his ass from the rear.

About 11am, I finally was able to break out. My daddy had two more services at noon and four but since I was Ms. Washington and not MRS. Washington I wasn't even ABOUT to sit around all day. I knew once my daddy finally left church he was gonna do what he always did on Sunday's now and head out to Michelle and Will's house for Sunday dinner. So I went home and got undressed, grabbed a glass of wine and some popcorn and got comfortable on the sofa watching lifetime movies. My plan was to chill and enjoy the silence until it was time for me to head out Laurel to pick up my kids from their father. Then an unfamiliar number came through on my cell and shit changed.

At first I thought it was Meeko on some fuck shit, calling me from somebody else number to try and catch me off guard so I let it go to voicemail. Ten minutes later I checked it and was surprised to find it was Chico. He left me a message that was so awkward that it was cute. He said he had got my number from Alana and was calling to see if I was busy later. And if I wasn't busy, he would love to take me to dinner. All of this came by way of him talking in circles and fumbling over his words. I was flattered. Flattered that he had the balls to step to me, KNOWING who I had dealings with. Although I was sure Alana had gave him the scoop before she parted with my number… not the whole horrid story of course but I knew she had put his ass on to me being single now.

I waited a whole hour before I called him back because I wasn't trying to seem desperate and shit. I was learning that niggas pay attention to shit like how soon you call and stuff and they use that as a guide on how to treat your ass. I wasn't about to make the same mistake twice. Chico and

I talked for about another hour and I agreed to let him come and scoop me at 8 and take me to dinner. As soon as I hung up with him, I called Meeko and asked him to keep the kids another night and I would just grab them from school the next day.

Lord, why did I do that? One would think since I had been in church that morning, the Lord would've ordered my steps, but he let me walk out on my own free will and that shit blew up off the break.

He started off fake grilling me about why I didn't answer him all the times he had hit me up the night before and why all of a sudden, I was <u>ABANDONING</u> my kids now. I wasn't trying to go through the bullshit he was throwing my way no more so I hung up on his ass. I knew this nigga like the back of my hand and knew that me hanging up on him alone was enough to piss him smooth the fuck off. So now he was gonna try to ruin my night by bringing the kids home IMMEDIATELY. I wasn't on that shit at all so I decided to beat him at his own game.

I hopped up, cleaned up my dishes and shit, threw on some sweats and a T shirt, grabbed an outfit for dinner with Chico and jetted on that ass. I started to go down my mother house, but she was still sitting in the Meeko cheering section so I knew if I went there or called her ass she was gonna do me just like Anna Mae mammy did and call the same nigga I was trying to get the fuck away from. So I went with plan B. I drove out Greenbelt and got me a room at the Marriot.

I chilled in my room, smoked a lil something, watched some TV and then called Chico and told him that I would meet him at the restaurant at 9pm instead of him picking me up.

I wanted to take a bubble bath so bad, but this was a hotel so I settled for a shower while bumping some Essences. While I was chilling and getting myself together and right for the night, it dawned on me that aside from that time down in Atlanta a few years back, I had never had a chance to live alone. It felt nice to just lay back with no kids, no dad and no man in my space. I smoked my weed in peace and thought about how different my shit could have been. Don't get me wrong, I loved Mikey and Mykia more than life itself BUT my decision to get involved with Meeko and have Mikey curved a lot of rites of passage for your girl and it had never dawned on me until this very moment. I decided right then, sitting on the bed butt ass naked in the Marriot blowing smoke that although I couldn't change the fact that I had kids, I could change a lot of the directions in my life. I vowed to never live with another nigga I wasn't married to for starters. It was time for me to have my own fucking space and know the joys of the child that truly has its own. That was just the start. For years I had dreams and goals but never truly voiced them but as of today that shit was changing. It was now MY TIME.

I got dressed in a pair of Parasugo jeans that look like they had been painted on me, a cream colored sweater and a pair of black Manolo boots. I let my hair hang long and loose that night, grabbed my purse and my keys and hit the door. I sashayed through the hotel and out to the parking lot to claim my vehicle and I was feeling myself as I turned heads all the way. All of this was simply boosting a bitch back up because I swear the last few months being with Meeko and the way things ultimately ended, I was feeling like a true fucking mud duck. I knew it wasn't true but after having two children, and a being with a man that had NEVER kept shit 100 with me, I was starting to question myself. So all the attention I was getting that night let me know that I truly wasn't the problem…. Meeko ass was. I hopped on in my Escalade and headed up the street to meet Chico.

We had agreed to meet at Jaspers and when I pulled into the parking space, I spotted him standing right out front waiting for me. Looking yummy as a motherfucka. He was even sweet enough to bring me flowers. It was a dozen roses but each one was a different color. He said he didn't know what my favorite color was so he decided to try them all until he figured it out. I thought it was extremely sweet that he cared about what my favorite color was. I wrapped my arms around his neck and kissed him softly on his cheek and you know what.... It felt good. I was glad to be there with him and he was glad to be there with me.

We went inside and grabbed a table. We ordered drinks and just fell into endless conversation. I was a lot more comfortable with him than I was the night before and vice versa. We talked about the neighborhood and all kinds of foolishness from back in the day. From fights, to hook ups, to robberies and who got killed when and by who. It was like hanging out with an old friend, then he dropped a bomb on me. He told me that he had a major crush on me back in the day. From the first time he saw me at the rec he wanted me to be his girl. I was blushing like crazy listening to him tell me how he used to try and push up his nerves to come and holler at me back in the day when he used to see me and my girls out and about. The crazy thing was, he told me the day he had finally worked up his nerves to come and talk to me, he was on his way to my house when he saw Meeko on the porch and I let him in. He said he saw that all my folks cars were gone so he kinda already knew what that meant. He said he sat on the corner of Neal street and watched and waited in his father's car he was driving for hours hoping he was wrong about what he was thinking. Then he finally saw Meeko leave out hours later and my peoples pulled up. We all know that was the day I lost my virginity. Now just think, if Chico hadn't been scared to step to me all that fucking time Meeko was locked up my story may have been a tad bit different. But we were here together now and that was all that mattered.

I damn near split my side laughing when he told me it took everything in him not to snitch my ass out to my parents when he saw them come home. But as I had just said, none of that even mattered now. All that mattered was that we were here together at this moment in time and everything about it felt so right.

The restaurant closed at midnight and that's when we left. We walked outside hand in hand, both smiling from ear to ear, completely pleased with the way our date had gone. It was clear neither of us was ready to say good night when I looked up and we had been standing in the parking lot an additional 25 minutes talking. I normally didn't move like this, but I felt 100% comfortable inviting him back to my room to chill. He got in his car and I got in my truck and he followed me back down the street to the Marriot.

Once we got in the room, I could tell he was a little nervous. I guess he did better with a crowd. We sat on the sofa in my room and had conversation about nothing important as I rolled up and sparked my good night blunt. We sat and put the smoke in rotation in complete silence. I was trying not to laugh but I could clearly see that he was in his own head hyping himself up to go for what he had been lusting after for years. But he aint have to worry because I had already made up my mind that he was getting this pussy tonight. I mean why the fuck else would I have invited him back to my room? Damn sure not to talk. We could've done that shit over the phone.

I got tired of waiting on him to find his inner beast and come get this pussy, so I got up and walked over to him and parked my ass right in his lap. His dick instantly felt like it was gonna bust through his jeans. I stood up in front of him and slowly took off every stitch of clothing I had on then sashayed over to the bed and laid back making sure my pussy was facing him. He was speechless and aint know how the fuck to take me at the moment. Once I got to making circles around my swollen clit with my index and middle finger he snapped out of his trance and realized he was invited to this party too.

I guess Chico ass had been playing the role because homebody walked over to the bed, grabbed my little ass and flipped me over on my stomach and ate my pussy from behind in a way that should have been against the law. You talking about climbing the walls, a bitch was stone cold breathless and lightheaded when he got finished with me. He had my ass RUNNING, head hanging off the other side of the motherfucking bed trying to get away from that trap he called a tongue. But he wouldn't let me loose for nothing. This motherfucka wrapped an arm around me and pulled my ass right back every single time I tried to get away. I aint have shit else left to give when he finally let my ass go, stood up, got butt ass naked, slipped on a condom and told my ass to turn over. I did exactly what he said, hell I aint have no choice. This nigga had me in a trance as he slid up in me and pounded my shit out.

Yep Chico ass had game and the way he put it to me in that room that night, a bitch was here to play for as long as he wanted me too…. Or until he started fucking up which unfortunately didn't take very long at all.

When I woke up the next morning, it was after 10am, so I had officially missed another day from school. I had to get a handle on that shit

ASAP. Chico had ordered us room service breakfast which I thought was sweet. We sat and ate together and then he hit me with a question from way out in left field. He asked me "What did last night mean?" I can't even stunt, that shit caught me off guard because well, that's not the type of nigga I was used to dealing with. He might as well had passed me a note that said "Can I have a chance? Check yes or no." Being a person who face always tells what they are thinking, I guess my confusion was echoing in the room. He stepped it up and told me flat out he wanted me, he always wanted me and he really wanted us to give us a chance. I sat and stared at him for a whole two minutes and no words were spoken. I was trying to read him because this was truly not what I was expecting. It was too soon truthfully speaking, but yet and still I found myself saying "Okay, we can give us a try." The truth of the matter was when I looked in his eyes, I didn't see any game or bullshit. Him stating that he wanted me was filled with sincerity and I hadn't experienced that before. While I had my share of niggas, none of them had every looked at me the way Chico was looking at me and that made me want to go with the flow. So I did. I was now officially Chico's girl.

We finally left the hotel around noon and went our separate ways but I had to leave him with the promise he could come and see me later on. When I got in my truck I checked my cell and I had 27 missed calls and 14 messages. 1 from my mother, 1 from my Father, and 1 from Alana…. The rest was from Meeko. This dude called me all kinds of no good ass whores, washed up trick ass bitches. He told me I would NEVER see my kids again and managed to threaten to take my life in every other sentence. I couldn't help but laugh because he was being fucking ridiculous and he knew it. I hadn't done a bit more than he had been doing the entire fucking time we knew each other. Only difference was I had the decency to wait until we were broke the fuck up before I started doing me. This nigga was fucking other bitches and would come home and eat my dinner and lay next to me like it was nothing from the very first time we lived together.

I went home to my Dad's house and took a shower, ate a sandwich and changed clothes and headed to Alana's house to kill time. She was on me from the moment I hit the door wanting to know about my date with Chico. I was surprised at myself as I found myself blushing over this nigga as I told her how things had gone down from hello to will you be my girl. Alana was happy for me and you know what, I was happy for myself. That happiness threatened to flee when Alana reminded me that Meeko was not going to take this shit lying down. How dare I move on. Who the fuck did I really think I was. Truth be told, I knew it wasn't gonna be no cake walk. True enough he was gonna bring me drama BUT Meeko's pride was a motherfucka. The same way he eventually stop sweating me and Santana being friends because his pride and ego wouldn't allow him to continue to devote time to caring out in the open….. I was expecting the same shit to happen with me and Chico. I finally rolled out a little after 4pm to go pick up my kids. Mikey loved his after school program so I would usually let him stay til about 5, then I would grab him and head over to Mykia's daycare.

I got to Mikey's school only to find him not at Aftercare because apparently, my baby wasn't in school at all that day. I didn't even explode because I already knew Meeko was gonna start playing games based on his messages. I was a little pissed that he had me waste gas and shit driving all the way out Laurel for nothing. I left Mikey's school and headed straight to Meeko house. Wasn't no point in going to Mykia school. The driveway at the house was empty, so I hopped out my truck and went up to the house and tried my keys…. Only to discover this negro had changed the locks. I went and sat back in my truck and tried to wait patiently. I ended up playing the callbot role myself. I called his ass 34 times and he didn't answer one time. I knew his dumb ass was playing tit for tat, but that aint help me NOT find myself growing angrier and angrier with each passing phone call and each passing minute.

Finally, I called Inda. Although she was my other Ma, we hadn't spoke like that since I caught Meeko and the bitch in the club together. I truly loved Inda, but I was at a point in my life where I was tired of hearing motherfuckas make excuses for and dismiss Meeko's trifling ass behavior. But I broke down and called her. She claimed she had talked to Meeko earlier in the morning when he was dropping the kids off at school and that he hadn't said anything about going back to get them. Now either she was lying for him as usual or he was lying to her also because I knew damn well they hadn't been to school. Next I called Gerald and he said he hadn't talked to him at all that day. I believed him because one thing Gerald didn't do was lie to me for Meeko. He claimed me as his daughter and refused to be mixed up in the middle of our shit trying to keep people lies and whatnot together.

While I was talking to Gerald, his actual daughters Niecee and Jacee chimed in on my line for a three way call. While we were talking, they hipped me to the fact that they were not talking to Inda. Apparently, Meeko the White Girl Slayer had brought his snow bunny to Sunday dinner at

Inda's. Now Jacee and Niecee both held issue with interracial dating and wanted no parts of it. They hadn't held their tongues on their opinions all their lives, so why Inda and Meeko thought that was gonna be the move escapes me. Things got pretty heated because as they always did, they spoke their minds. Not only was he foul for bringing home a whole bitch his family fell apart over BUT she was Melanin deficient to boot. They said he was pissed and took her and our kids and left, then Inda jumped in their asses and now they weren't talking to her at all.

While I loved Inda, Jacee and Niecee I honestly didn't give too fucks about them not speaking. I couldn't get my mind off the fact that he had this bitch around my children. The kid gloves were now off. Meeko was 100% free to do whatever it was he chose to do. But what I was not gonna stand for by any stretch of the imagination was this negro taking my children around ANY bitch. I refused to let him subject my babies to a fucking revolving door of whores that was surely in the making. My children had a stellar mother and wasn't no bitch about to try and play step mom to mine. I wasn't having it.

I guess my level of pisstivity was shinning through so Niecee hung up and left me and Jacee on the phone and I was going through the motions. Jacee kept trying to call her back on the three way but she wasn't answering. About 15 minutes later, Niecee was pulling up in the driveway behind me. I was in the middle of a true breakdown. Like why the fuck was he doing this to me? Like seriously, what had I ever done to Meeko to deserve constant bullshit?

Niecee hopped in the truck with me and was my shoulder to cry on, and cry I did. It's truly some kinda hurt you feel when a nigga not only replaces you as his woman BUT THEN tries to replace you as a mother to your children. We sat there in Meeko's driveway until about 9:30pm, that's when his G Wagon pulled up, followed by a Nissan Maxima. Niecee and I both got out my truck just as he stepped out of his and his snow bunny Jenna hopped out the Maxima. Before he could even fully grasp what was happening, I had pulled a football shuffle and took off through the grass and was on Jenna's ass. I grabbed this bitch by her hair and slung her to the ground and commenced to giving her the business. I was in a dark place and all that hurt I had been toting around was coming out and poor Jenna was catching it. I don't know how long I was wailing on this bitch, but I certainly remembered when Meeko intervened. He snatched me off of her and threw me to the ground breaking me out of my ass whopping trance.

"What the fuck is wrong with you Mikki!" Meeko yells at Mikki in anger while standing over top of her.

Mikki jumps up and mushes him in his face with all her might. "Keep that fucking slut ass bitch the fuck away from kids Meeko! I swear to God this shit will get worse and worse!"

"You sound dumb as shit! Them my fucking kids too and they'll be around whoever the fuck I take them around!"

"Okay then motherfucka, YOU wont fucking see them anymore PERIOD!" Mikki takes a telegraphed swing at Meeko. He blocks the punch and pushes her down in the grass. "Where the fuck are my kids Meeko?!"

"Why you care bitch? You wasn't worried about them yesterday when you ditched them to go and get fucked whore!"

"I was at my fucking sister house dumb bitch!" Mikki yells, telling a bold face lie.

"Bitch you lying! Your fucking mother called over there and they said they hadn't seen your skeezeball ass since you left church bitch!" Meeko snap, now knowing that Mikki is indeed seeing someone else because of her need to lie about where she was.

Mikki gets up off the ground and gets back in Meeko's face. "And if I did, how is that your fucking business? You running around with this bitch and only God knows who else. I will do whatever the fuck I please!"

"Bitch I don't give a fuck what you do! Go ahead and be the whore you been aspiring to be since the day I met your motherfucking ass!" Mikki charges Meeko and he grabs her up and slams her against his truck. "Mikki, I'm not trying to hurt you, so please, just get the fuck away from my house before I call the police on you."

"You gonna call the police on me huh?" Mikki chuckles

"Hell Yeah!" Meeko lets her go. "You out here

acting a fucking fool, being loud and ghetto for no fucking reason. Take that shit back around Trinidad somewhere before I do like I said and call the police on your ass. That's if one of my neighbors aint already called them on your ass!"

"Fuck you AND you neighbors bitch!" Mikki hock spits right in Meeko's face.

Meeko instantly flips and slaps Mikki as hard as he can before grabbing her and flinging her back down to the ground. He attempts to continue his all out assault on her but Niecee jumps on his back and begins hitting him, causing him to have to try and fight off both women. He finally is able to flip Niecee over his shoulder and she falls to the ground. "Bitch you gonna take this ho ass bitch side over your own fucking brother!" Meeko looks at his sister in disbelief, caught somewhere between being angry and being hurt.

"Fuck you Meeko! You dead ass wrong for this shit!" Niecee screams on him.

"I'm wrong because I don't want her tired ass nomore? Yo, I swear to God you a stupid bitch just like her. Get the fuck off my property. Bitch you dead to me!" Meeko walks over to Jenna's car, where she has now locked herself inside of as a way to protect herself from Mikki. She unlocks the door and Meeko takes her hand and helps her out. They begin to walk to the house with him somewhat acting as a shield to her.

Mikki takes off as they get to the front stairs and grabs Jenna by her hair again, pulling her from Meeko's protection and begins to beat on her again. Meeko grabs Mikki by her neck and begins to choke her down to the ground until she has spit coming out the sides of her mouth and is clawing at his hands trying to get free from his grip. As soon as Jenna gets the front door open to the house, Meeko finally lets Mikki go. He walks away from her and leaves her on the ground coughing, hacking and struggling to breathe. He stops when he gets inside the front door and turns to face Mikki. "I'm telling you now Mikki, just go ahead and get the fuck away from my house. I don't want you. Run back to that nigga you was with last night because we finished. If you come to my house again, I swear to God I'm gonna kill you with my bare fucking hands Mikki. I promise you this." Meeko turns around and slams his front door and locks it. Niecee gets up off the ground and comes over to help Mikki, who is now laying on the ground crying tears of sadness as Meekos words continue to bounce around in her head.

"I was so hurt by Meeko shit, I couldn't even see straight. What's crazy is that all that fighting we had done out there, that wasn't the pain I felt. The pain I felt came solely from his words. Niecee was trying to get me to come on and leave, but they had managed to block me in when they pulled into the driveway. My head was so heavy with embarrassment as I walked up to the house that I used to call my own and had to ring the doorbell in order to ask the same motherfucka that had just told me he didn't want me to please move him and his girlfriend vehicles so that I could take my broken heart on home to my fathers house. Yeah that was a hard pill to swallow.

After I rang the bell twice, Meeko opened the door and threw an arm full of my shit in my face then slammed it. I stood there in total shock, not knowing what to say or do at this moment. I didn't want to cry because being a woman, I knew Jenna was in there watching me from the safety of the house, and letting another bitch see you break was a no-no. But I was so fucked up, I couldn't stop the tears if I wanted to.

Niecee came and pulled me from the front door to her car which was parked on the street. We watched in horror as Meeko continued to make trips to the front door, straight throwing my shit out on the lawn like I was just a regular-smegular bitch to him. Not the chick he asked to marry him at one point in time. Not the chick that gave birth to his pride (Mikey) and his joy (Mykia). Not the chick that held him the fuck down while he was locked up when all them other bitches he played me for stepped off. Not the chick who was all out of state setting niggas up for his ass because he wanted that spot. None of that shit mattered as he continued to embarrass my ass tossing my shit in the grass while the whole neighborhood looked on from their windows and some even came and stood out on their porches shaking their heads at the foolishness being displayed. After the yard was littered with all my shit, I finally found the strength to speak and all it did was push shit from bad to worse.

"Your lawn decorations are cute Meeko. But you can keep them clothes and shit. Can I just get my money please?"

"What fucking Money?" Meeko asks, ready to smack the shit out of Mikki at this point.

Mikki walks across the yard littered with her clothes and stops before she gets to the stairs where Meeko is standing. "I just want my money that's downstairs please." Meeko chuckles in disbelief knowing exactly what money she is asking about. "Marissa, please get the fuck on away from me."

"But I need my money Meeko."

"Fuck you alright!" Meeko screams in her face.

"I need my money Meeko! That's my shit and I earned every fucking cent of it putting up with your trifling ass! I need my money to take care of my kids and pay for school!" Mikki yells through her tears.

"Mikki fuck you and your tears. Fuck your school and fuck what you talking about. That's my fucking money. You aint earn shit. Bitch I spent three fucking years of my life locked the fuck away because of your ho ass!"\

"Nigga you chose to take that charge and…."

"Bitch I did that shit for you! Because I loved your ho ass!" Meeko shoves Mikki to the ground. "Mikki please, just get the fuck away from me! I hate your ass!"

Mikki continues to cry while sitting on the ground. "Meeko I need my money to pay for school!"

Meeko looks at her wearing a mask of both anger and hurt. "You wanna go to school Mikki, go sell some more pussy like you did last night to pay your tuition because I'm the fuck done with your ass." Meeko walks in his house and slams the door, locks it and sets his alarm.

Mikki finally gets up off the ground and Niecee helps her begin to pick up her clothes off the ground. They start to put the clothes in the back of Mikki's Escalade when Meeko comes running back out the house. He runs over to the truck and snatches the keys out the ignition. Mikki runs from the back of the truck and starts wrestling him for the keys. "Give me my shit Meeko! You not taking my fucking truck!"

"Bitch I brought this truck, get home the best fucking way you can!"

"Meeko you going too damn far and you know it!" Niecee yells at him.

"Fuck you too trader bitch." Meeko closes all the doors and locks the truck setting the alarm. He takes the keys to Ike's house off and throws them at Mikki. "Like I said, get the nigga you ran off to fuck last night to make sure you got wheels, and tuition money and all the other shit I did for your ho ass. Now for the last time get the fuck off my property because when I go in and close my door, if yall still here, I'm calling the fucking police."

"Well bitch you might as well call them right now!" Mikki turns and starts kicking dents in Jenna's car. Meeko walks away and goes in his house and closes the door. Mikki circles Jenna's car kicking dents in it just as four Prince George's County squad cars pull up in front of the house.

"When I saw the flashing lights of those police cars, shit kinda got real for me. I dropped to my knees and started bawling crying. Meeko had taken everything from me AND called the police on me. Like seriously, who has the mother of their children arrested? Especially when they are the cause of her actions. Niecee was trying to explain the situation but they wasn't too much giving a fuck. Two of them went up to Meeko's

house and Jenna let them inside, while I was handcuffed and placed in the back of a police car. The officer asked me what happened and you know what was crazy, while I was trying to talk my way out of a trip to jail, I found myself sub consciously trying to protect Meeko. I didn't want him to go to jail for the way he attacked me out in his yard or nothing, so I was talking all around that. Mainly crying though and trying to convince them it was all a big ass misunderstanding.

Ten minutes later the other officers came back out the house and my ass was going to jail.

I broke down in the back of the police car and cried like a baby. Meeko had taken everything from me at this point. My home, my car, my kids and even my damn money. After all we had been through together, after all I had done for his ass, this is how it ended.

I was released the next morning with a summons to come back to court in two weeks. Niecee was there to pick me and deliver the news that Mikey and Mykia were fine. Santana had called my phone while I was locked up wanting to know what time I was picking them up. Apparently, Meeko had dropped them off with her Monday morning instead of taking them to school. I was too exhausted to even wrap my mind around the why of all the shit he was doing. I hadn't slept or nothing. Santana met us at my dad's house with my kids and told me the full story of Meeko dropping them off claiming that something bad had happened to one of my sisters and I would be to get them later. That shit just pissed me off all over again. Not only do you hide my fucking kids from me, but straight out lie on my family and shit while doing so. He had me HOT once again. I could tell Santana felt caught in the middle of our bullshit, although I wasn't the one that put her there. He did. She kept trying to convince me to give him some time and things would cool off, but I was over that shit. This motherfucka did what he wanted, when he wanted, and with WHO he wanted our whole relationship. But when I finally move the fuck on, I'm everything but a child of God.

Santana was working hard to convince me that Meeko was just being the same Meeko he had always been, and you know what, she was right to an extent. Only difference was I was DONE putting up with his shit. Since he wanted to play dirty, I was gonna give him exactly what he wanted.

I was glad my dad was gone to New York for the week on business. I wasn't in the mood to explain what was going on now. I was especially glad when I walked in the bathroom to take a shower and saw my damn face. I don't know when I had gotten it, but I had a huge bruise on my left cheek. It felt like the minute I saw it, it all of a sudden started to sting like hell. I grabbed my phone to use the camera on it. I stripped down and took pictures of my face and arms that were bruised up from the way Meeko had done me. Seeing that shit broke me on the inside and pissed me completely off in the same breath. I felt a hatred for Meeko that I didn't know I could possess. That warm and fuzzy feeling I used to get when I thought of his ass was now replaced with ice water. He did me so dirty and I decided right then I was gonna trump his dirty ASAP.

The next morning I called Niecee and asked her to babysit for me because I didn't want to take them all the way out Laurel to school. Besides I had a mission to complete and wasn't sure I was even gonna be finished dealing with this shit in time to pick them up on time, so keeping them out of school was my best bet. Throw in the fact I didn't even have wheels anymore and I would've been a fool to take them all the way out there. Niecee said she would come and get them so I fed them and got us all ready. I didn't wear makeup but managed to find some left behind by one of my sisters and used some foundation to cover up my bruises. I went downstairs in my dad's office and emailed myself the pictures from my phone of the bruises Meeko had left me with and printed them out. As soon as I had the pictures in my hand, Niecee was calling me to say she was outside so I grabbed the kids and everything I needed for this day and headed out the door. I had her drop me off at the Metro station and told her I would pick the kids up about 8pm. I could tell she was nervous about whatever I had planned for the day partially because I wouldn't disclose what was on my to do list. I just said I was taking care of my situation and left it at that. Niecee was my boo but at the end of the day she was still Meeko's sister and I would've been a damn fool to disclose my plans for the day, and while I had walked around with my dunce cap on for years…. That bitch was off now and in the whole fucking trash.

I hadn't been on the train in what felt like a million years, but I hopped on the orange line at Stadium-Armory and hopped off at metro center and jumped on the red line and rode it to Judiciary Square. I never though the day would come when I would need to do the shit I was down here to do but I was done letting my love for Meeko guide how I dealt with him and all his bullshit.

I spent the morning in the court building filing for an order of protection against Meeko. I had no idea how the process worked and didn't want to call my mother beforehand and ask her because I didn't want her singing Meeko praises and telling me how the fuck I was overreacting. I was thinking the pictures of the bruises and the messages he left me threatening my life would have been enough to have them issue the shit on sight, but it didn't work that way. After I filled out the paperwork, I had to go and stand in open court and give descriptive details of the incident that had transpired between Meeko and I. The shit was embarrassing because everybody that was sitting in the courtroom would know your business and that shit aint sit right with me. I also found myself standing in open court telling a bold face lie. I couldn't tell a judge in Washington, DC that I had took my ass out to Laurel, to a house I no longer lived in, assaulted his bitch, spit in his face and kicked big ass dents in that woman vehicle. Oh hell no. The narrative I gave went something like this……

Meeko had the kids for the weekend and I went out with friends. When he brought them home, I hadn't got there yet so he waited until the next day and jumped on me after hiding my kids from me at someone elses house I didn't know and refusing to return them, saying he would kill them first.

I felt bad about lying like that on him, but fuck that. Shit had changed, and I wanted his ass barred from contacting me or my kids since he wanted to carry shit the way he was carrying it. So I did what I had to do to get what I wanted. The judge granted me a temporary protective order and a court date for the following month. Next I headed down to the family court floor and filed for sole physical custody of my kids as well as child support.

Now filing that shit was hard for a number of reasons, and I found myself sheading real live tears during this ordeal. I remembered back when I got pregnant with Mikey, after we tried to get the abortion and found out we couldn't, Meeko was so happy about becoming a dad. Mikey was his world from the moment he sucked air into those tiny lungs, hell even before that. And Mykia... he adored this little girl and her little ass felt the same for him. I sat there with tears rolling down my face as I thought about the relationship he had with our kids. Don't get me wrong, he loved Santana and Liz's daughters also, but I think because Mykia and Mikey were mine he loved them differently if that makes sense. It really hurt because NEVER did I think shit would end up here with us. Meeko and I had broken up more than once and he always still made sure Mikey and I were straight, but shit was different now. Lines had been crossed. This man went weeks without even speaking to our children after we went to LA. How was I really supposed to trust him to keep making sure they were straight? And keep in mind I was moving the fuck on with my life, so this shit was different than before. I think if he had just given me my money and let me get the fuck on about my business I wouldn't have been going this route but what real choice did the nigga leave me?

Here I was with two kids, no job, no car, no place of my own. Hell I couldn't even finish school because he was playing with my fucking money. I had NEVER received government assistance and I wasn't about to start now. Meeko had taken care of us and until I was able to get my shit together or he ran me my fucking money, he was STILL gonna take of us…. By choice or by force, it was up to him BUT the shit was gonna be done. And right now with the shit he was doing seemed to me like the nigga was choosing FORCE.

I left the court building with two court dates and a temporary protection against Meeko. I walked down to Archives and hopped on the yellow line and rode the train out to Regan National Airport and rented me a car since I didn't have wheels of my own and this motherfucka was holding my money hostage. Thank God I had sense enough to have a few credit cards. I had been responsible with them since day one because my goal was to keep building my credit so that I could do shit. Yeah a bitch had plans and while Meeko had money, it wasn't like we could go around buying shit outright without the IRS and a slew of other three letter combination agencies looking like ….. hold up, wait a minute. What the fuck are they really doing over there? Shit the house out in Laurel was in Inda's name, and while I loved her I wasn't trying to live my whole life running around with shit in her name. I wanted my shit in my own name. So I was determined to get to that level where we could use my name and his money without motherfuckas looking at us sideways. Fuck y'all thought I was pushing through school so hard for? Cause I refused to end up a bitch in cuffs sitting down because she had never done shit with her life, had no credit whatsoever BUT lived in a big ass house and drove an over priced car and the shit didn't add up in the eyes of the law.

So while Meeko bitched and moaned about me being in school, his dumb ass couldn't see that shit was to help US in the long run. Before shit went left I had plans to become Meeko's wife. I wanted that club out his father's name, as well as those cars. I wanted our shit to belong to us. So me finishing school and opening my business was gonna create the perfect front to mask the money this nigga constantly brought in and was spending. But he was too busy running around beating his chest about his woman being at home cooking and cleaning and ironing that he couldn't see the forest for the trees. So fuck it and him.

I copped my rental Dodge Magnum and headed back to the city. I finally called Chico back because he had been hitting me up since the night he was supposed to come through to see me, but I was busy getting locked the fuck up. We talked for a minute, I told him I had some shit pop off but kept it brief. I didn't need him knowing the extent of how ugly shit had gotten between me and Meeko. True I agreed to give a relationship with him a chance, but my business was still my business all day long. Besides, his ass probably would've ran for the hills had he known me and Meeko were in the middle of an all out war with each other. Anyway, I agreed to let him come and see me that night. Next, I went to the post office and paid to have two certified letters sent to Meeko at Inda's house. Meeko was rarely home when we lived together so I couldn't expect the mailman to catch his ass out Laurel, but somebody was always at Inda's house and they could sign for the shit if need be so that's where I sent his court summons to.

I headed over to Niecee's house to pick up my kids but ended up chilling with her for a bit. I went on and told her what the deal was because wasn't no point in hiding the shit. She would find out what was going on when he got the shit in the mail anyway. To my surprise she understood and was like she would've done the same thing with him carrying on the way he was doing these days. We were in agreement that this bitch had him feeling himself. As if on cue, my phone rung and it was Meeko. I laughed because I was thinking damn, did this nigga have me wired and heard what we were talking about. I knew damn well he hadn't received his paperwork that fast, so I went on and answered. I figured I might as well let him know that if he called me again he could find himself back in that dreaded 6x9 so go sit the fuck on down somewhere. It was only fair."

"Hello." Mikki answers calmly.

"Where you at?" Meeko asks as if he hadn't just treated her like shit two days before.

"Why? What's Up?"

"Look, I need to see you. Like immediately."

"The fuck for?"

"Because we need to talk."

"Nah, that ship has sailed."

"Fuck you mean it's sailed?"

"Exactly what I said. Besides if you came near me you would technically be in violation. As a matter of fact, this call alone is a violation. I just answered to let you know what's really good."

'Yeah. And what's that Mikki?" Meeko asks with a chuckle.

"So today I went and got a temporary restraining order and filed for sole custody of the kids." Mikki responds matter-of-factly.

"Bitch you gone mad. Mikki stop playing with me."

"That's the thing Meeko, I have stopped playing with you which is why I am doing what I need to do to protect my children and myself."

"Yo Mikki, this your final chance to cut the shit before I roll up on your ass."

"This is exactly why I went and did what I did."

"Bitch you think a funky ass piece of paper gonna stop me? The fuck is wrong with you?"

"Michael, if that paper wont stop you, I guarantee MPD the fuck will."

"Yeah we gonna see."

"Sir, please do not call this number anymore or I will be forced to report the violation to the proper authorities." Mikki says with extreme calm causing Meeko to lose his cool.

"You slut ass bitch, you think what I did to your ass the other night was something, wait til I run down on your ass this time. Bitch I promise I'ma put a fucking bullet in your ho ass head. I put that on my fucking kids bitch!"

"Michael, you do what you feel you need to do. Your summons as well as your copy of my protective order should be arriving in the mail as early as tomorrow. You have received verbal notice and that is the physical notice. The authorities have copies of the threating messages you left me Sir, so if something happens to me they know exactly who to pick up… keep in mind you already have two strikes Sir, do you REALLY want a third?" Mikki asks in a matter-of-fact tone.

"BITCH…." Meeko explodes as Mikki hangs up the phone on him.

"Niecee and I were dying laughing at him flipping completely the fuck out, but while we were laughing at this nigga in all his rage, we wasn't no fucking fools. So, on that note I grabbed my kids and got ghost. I mean, I was hoping and praying that while he would be fuming mad, he wasn't dumb enough to disregard the fact that he was on Parole in the State of Maryland. So if he got picked up on some bullshit in DC there was a great chance they would step his ass right back. While we all knew that could become his reality, the fact was that he was pissed clean the fuck off right now and liable to take that risk if he needed to. Some shit could make a motherfucka mad enough to eat 7 years like its nothing, and while I hoped that this wasn't one of those things for him, there was a chance that it could be. I mean he did threaten to put a whole fucking bullet in my head. So, I couldn't call it and I wasn't about to take that shit lightly.

I got the kids some Wendy's and headed home. I parked my rental on Neal Street and walked around the corner because I didn't know if Meeko was gonna come through or not and didn't want to tip him off that I had wheels now. I knew him well enough to know he would attribute any new wheels on the block to me, so I was hiding my rental until further notice.

By 10pm, my kids were finally sleep and Chico was calling me to let me know he was on the way over. I decided to change plans because my father had came back early. So with him being home and the thought that Meeko could be sitting around watching the house, I decided to have Chico meet me. After I hoe bathed in the sink and slipped on a pair a pair of sweatpants and a t shirt I asked my dad to listen out for the kids and rolled out. Me and Chico ended up meeting at Woodridge park up on 18th street. This put us far enough away from the neighborhood where I wasn't worried about anybody spotting us together. I had decided I was gonna fuck him and then go ahead and cut him off. It wasn't his fault, but I knew shit was only gonna get worse between Meeko and me and I wasn't tryna have nobody else caught up in my shit.

When I got to the park, Chico was already sitting there waiting for me in his Suburban. I got out my rental and jumped in the truck with him. He already had a freshly rolled blunt waiting for me. I knew then it was gonna be hard to let him go."

Mikki adjust her seat then leans over and kisses Chico on the cheek. "Damn you got here fast."

"I was around the way when I called you so I aint

have far to go. Chico sparks the blunt, takes a pull and blows it out. He passes it to Mikki and she falls back in her seat and takes a long pull.

"You must have known I needed this."

"Yeah, you sounded stressed, so I figured I would try and help you ease that shit."

"I appreciate it baby."

"Don't thank me yet. A nigga aint done." Chico smiles wickedly at Mikki as she passes the blunt back to him.

"Is that right?" Mikki smiles matching his naughty thoughts.

"Yeah. So, you gonna come home with me tonight? I been thinking about that pussy all day Mikki."

"Is that right?" Mikki starts to gently caress her nipples through her thin t shirt causing them to swell twice their normal size.

"You have no idea boo."

"Then show me." Mikki demands seductively.

" I plan to. As soon as we get to the crib."

"What's wrong with right here?"

"Here? In my truck?" Chico asks, not really into public sex.

"Yes. Here. In Your truck." Mikki laughs as she takes her shirt off right there in the front seat. Chico looks on in shock and amazement as she slides out of her sweatpants showing that she isn't wearing any panties. Mikki climbs across over the seat into the back.

"Yo you wild as shit Mikki." Chico smiles as he passes her the blunt.

"I was about to get in my feelings thinking he was gonna turn me down cause you could clearly see his ass was scared. But he didn't. He

locked the doors, put the song that was bumping in the system, Bonita Applebum, on repeat and then climbed in the backseat with me.

One thing I definitely was loving about Chico was his desire to please me. I didn't even have to say anything. As soon as he got in the backseat with me, he took his shirt off, pulled me towards him by legs and proceeded to give me a tongue lashing that was out of this world. I laid back, inhaling KUSH while he went to work trying to suck my juice box dry. This nigga tongue was NOT A GAME AT ALL. He ate the pussy until I came, and kept right on going until I had to force his head away because I was about to burn my damn self with the blunt... either that or set his damn truck on fire. Neither was good, so even though the feeling he was giving a bitch was out of this world I had to stop him. Once I got myself together, I put the condom on him, climbed on top of him and rode his ass into backseat bliss.

This thing between Chico and I was really new, like not even a week old yet and I was digging him. But as I slid up and down his pole in the backseat of his truck, enjoying that sting of every ass slap he delivered while his mouth was filled with tiddies, all I could really focus on was what I came here to do this evening. It was becoming clear to me that because of my decision to tie myself to Meeko all those years ago, I was gonna have to miss out on something and someone that could've been perfect for me.

Once we were done, I laid on Chico's chest and just started crying. I didn't want to be boo-whooing over a nigga I just started rocking with. And technically it wasn't over him. It was over my own situation. Instead of looking at me like the crying fool I was, Chico comforted me... and that let me know what I had to do."

"Aye Mikki, you alright? What's wrong boo?"

"Chico you just don't understand."

"Then help me understand baby. I'm your man, so that's my job."

Mikki looks up at Chico and smiles through her tears. "Why you just didn't come on to my house that time back in the day Chico? My shit could've been so different now."

Chico kisses the top of her head. "You don't mean that shit Mikki. Everything worked out how it was supposed to back then. Y'all were meant to have yall time. Have y'all little ones together and now it's our time baby."

"I wish it was that simple." Mikki sits up and holds Chico's hand. "Chico, I'm really digging you and I really do want to see where this thing of ours goes. BUT, with everything going on between Meeko and Me right now…. I just…" Mikki drops her head as tears start to fall from her eyes again.

Chico lifts her head and kisses her softly. "You just what boo?"

"I just don't want to get you caught up in no shit that aint your issue to deal with. I don't know how Meeko gonna act when it gets to him that me and you rocking tough. I just got a restraining order against this nigga. He hot right now. And I just don't want to complicate your life with my bullshit because of who I chose to fuck with back in the day."

"So what you wanna keep shit low key between us?"

"If you are willing to."

"I can dig it. So we will keep us between us in the mean time until your shit is less complicated."

"Thank you for understanding Chico. You really are the best."

"It's my job to be." Chico moves in and kisses Mikki passionately.

"We sat in the backseat of his truck and made out for a few, long enough to get us both geared up for round two. I went on and gave in and followed him to his apartment out Hyattsville. We got it in again and then slept in each others arm. I got up about 5am and made my way back home. I wanted to get in before my Father or my kids woke up, but I had no such luck. When I walked in my dad was in the kitchen brewing his morning Coffee.

I swear, when he looked at me, I felt 14 and pregnant again. I was about ready to run upstairs and grab my kids and run for the bolt up out of there before he tried to put my ass on the fast track to boarding school again."

Ike looks at Mikki sneaking into his house at 5:30 in the morning. He takes a deep breath to control his anger and pulls out a chair from the kitchen table instructing his youngest daughter to come and have a seat without saying a word. Mikki walks over to the table and sits there, feeling like a child again as Ike finishes making his coffee. He makes her a cup also and then comes and sits at the table across from her. "Late night?" He asks, dripping with sarcasm.

"Daddy it wasn't like that. I went down Alana's house because she's having a hard time dealing with her break up and I fell asleep and…."

"I guess Alana gave you that big ole suck mark on your neck." Mikki grabs her neck in shock and embarrassment. Ike chuckles at her reaction. "There is nothing on your neck Marissa. But your reaction lets me know you just left a situation that could've left something on it."

Mikki lowers her eyes in shame. "Daddy, I…."

"Just listen to me Marissa. I know you are grown now and I can't do anything about you having a sex life. I'm just asking you to stop and think about the decisions you are out here making. You have two children, no husband, no job and sneaking in and out the house to go and lay up. What's wrong with that picture Marissa?"

"Everything." Mikki says as tears start to fall from her eyes.

"You weren't raised like this. I know I made a huge mistake when you came home pregnant back then. And had I not acted like an ass and been able to support you, a lot that followed more than likely wouldn't have. God saw fit to give you and I a second chance without all the outside influence, so I'm not gonna make the same mistake twice and turn against you in your time of need."

"I appreciate that daddy."

"However, I'm not gonna sit by idle and watch you fall further down the rabbit's hole."

"I know you not daddy."

"You're grown now, so it's only so much I can say or do. I just want to remind you that men treat you how you allow them to treat you. So if you show a man that you are the type of woman that is okay to call late at night, have her leave her children to come and lay up and then take the walk of shame in the morning, then baby girl, that's exactly how he is gonna treat you despite what he says."

"Daddy nothing happened between us. We watched movies and ended up falling asleep and that was it. I don't want to introduce him to the kids because this is still new, and I wasn't gonna invite him to your house because that's disrespectful to you and…."

"What's disrespectful about a man coming to your door, like a man, sitting inside your house watching a movie Mikki?"

"Nothing, I just thought."

"Marissa, I don't know what went on when your mother took you girls away from me. I'm not even going to ask because it's water under the bridge now. However, I need you to know you are a grown woman now need to act accordingly. And acting like a grown woman is so much more than spreading your legs.

"I know daddy."

"So, I will say this. Whoever this man is that got you sneaking out to watch all night movies…" Ike pauses to let the lie Mikki told linger in the air. "You let him know that if he wants to date you, he needs to come correct. He needs to come by here and ring the doorbell and ask for you by name… not Mikki, but Marissa because although they live in the same shell they are two different people. He needs to make my acquaintance, He needs to make your mother's acquaintance. He needs to call on Sunday to make plans for the upcoming Friday or Saturday night. He needs to take you on dates, get to know your likes and dislikes, what makes you smile, what makes you sad, what your passions are in life. Most importantly he needs to respect that you have two small children at home. Once you lay down this foundation Marissa, and excuse my language but close your legs, it will be easy for you to find the man that is for you, that God has sent for you and weed out all these suckas who only want to see what you look like laying down.

Ike grabs Mikki's hand and looks in her eyes sincerely. "Mikki you are my baby girl and I love you dearly. I never could have fathomed that some of the roads you have walked would have been yours. But they were and it is what it is. I don't know what went on between you and Michael, if you ever want to talk to me about it, you know my door is open not just as your pastor but as your father. I just don't want to see you make the same mistake again, investing time in a man that is not for you. I do hope you understand.

"I do daddy."

"And Mikki, if you ever wanna talk to about it, I'm right here.

"Okay daddy."

Ike kisses Mikki on her forehead. "I love you baby girl."

"I know daddy. I love you too." Mikki grabs Ike's hand. "Daddy, will you pray with me?"

"Of course, I will baby girl. Of Course, I will."

"Me asking my daddy to pray with me lit him up like a Christmas Tree. We stood in the kitchen, held hands and bowed our heads as he spoke to God on my behalf. When he was done, and we said our Amen, I went on upstairs to get myself and my children together for the day we had ahead of us. It was time to put some order back in our lives, starting with this restraining order against Meeko.

The first stop on my agenda was Mykia's school. I was trying to get them situated so that I could make it to class on time. I was gonna find a way to pay my tuition because not finishing was not an option. When I got to Mykia's school, I went straight to the director. I hated having to involve other people in my business, but this situation called for it. Without giving her all the torrid details, I let her know there was an issue between Meeko and I, so I now had a temporary restraining order against him that included my children, therefore he was NOT to pick her up anymore. She said she understood, made a copy of the order for Mykia's file and said she would inform her teachers. I thanked her, dropped my munchkin off in her classroom and then Mikey and I left headed to his school which is when things got a little more complicated.

After I saw my baby off to his class, I went to the Principal office and wanted to punch this bitch in the face by time I left. I gave her the same info I had given the director at Mykia's school and the original protection order so that she could make a copy of it. She looked it over and handed it back to me and told me that it was invalid in the state of Maryland. I'm like no it's not. And she's like they wouldn't honor an order of protection unless it was filed in the State of Maryland. She started rambling on about where I could go in Upper Marlboro to apply for one etc, but I was too pissed to hear her for real. Here I am telling you that the situation between he and I is so serious that he can't have any contact with his own fucking kids until further notice and you talking to me about some state line shit.

I had to will myself not to go slam off on this bitch. I was sure Meeko either knew or would do his homework and find out that my little piece of paper didn't mean shit in the state he resided and our children went to school. That meant that even with a protection order saying he was not to call me, email me, text me or come within 500 feet of my person, my residence or my children. It specifically named my dad's address, and each of my children's school. I was in my feelings because I'm thinking that if what this bitch was saying was true, why would DC include two addresses that are clearly across state lines? Why would Mykia's school accept it without question?

It didn't make sense to me and I wasn't even about to play with Meeko and these people. While in my heart I never thought he would do harm to our children intentionally, I did know he was spiteful enough to take my babies and get low on my ass. So I made the decision right then to pull Mikey and transfer him to a school in DC. I filled out the paperwork and signed everything then headed back to Mikey's classroom to get him.

He was PISSED when he found out what was going on. He loved his classmates and teachers, and I hated to do this to him, but I had to do what was best for all of us. He was too young to truly understand what was going on with our family, and although me and his father was engaged in an all-out war, I would never talk down on his name to our children. I drove back to Mykia's school watching Mikey have a whole fit in the backseat. Again, I felt bad for him but in this case, I had to make an executive decision in this matter. He would just have to learn to deal.

When we got to Mykia's school and I told the director I was gonna pull her, she understood. I explained to her why and because of the extreme circumstances, she was nice enough to waive the penalty that would've been imposed for withdraw without sufficient notice.

The rest of the day, I had to try to dance around Mikey's attitude and that shit was WORK. He had no understanding about being pulled out of school and when I explained that he was gonna be transferring, he really started to let them chromosomes that Meeko leant his ass show. Like I had to walk away from the boy on more than one occasion to keep from slamming his little ass.

I was trying my hardest to keep shit vague as far as why I was transferring him because again I never wanted to take anything away from the relationship Mikey had with Meeko. He real live adored his dad, and his dad felt the same way about him and his sister. It was ME that Meeko hated and continuously hurt. So as fucked up as Meeko was to me, I took all the venom from his son and took on the role as the bad guy in all of this. I was Mikey's mother, he was gonna forever love me, but I felt like relationships with fathers could be broken a lot easier. So to protect what they had, I bit the bullet…. Until the boy got beside himself.

I was letting the boy live until I caught him mumbling some oober slick shit under his breath. I didn't catch all of it, just the ass end about hating me and wishing I FUCKING DIE so that he could go live with his father. With all the sacrifices I made since the day I found out his big head ass had invaded my womb, that was my breaking point. I had been sitting on the floor in the living room playing with Mykia when he said that shit as he stomped off up the stairs. He didn't even make it to top before I was on his ass.

I hated hitting my child as a way to correct his behavior. I didn't believe in it for the most part. Like I'm an adult and you are a child… if the only way I can correct your behavior is to beat on you then I'm the one with the problem was how I saw it. My father preached spare the rod, spoil the child and while I understood it, I didn't agree with it. But this day was different. Mikey needed his ass bust and who was I to deny him??

The next day was another missed one for me where school was concerned. I needed to get Mikey situated at his new school which was Wheatley. It was literally eyeball distance from our front door so it was the obvious choice for him. Once he was enrolled and off to his new classroom, I went to see a few daycares I had inquired about for Mykia. I lucked up and the second one I saw I fell in love with. It wasn't too far from my dad's house. I used my credit card to pay the deposit and first month of tuition and was happy to have gotten that out of the way. I also knew I had to start looking for a job because while I wanted to finish school, being truthfully honest, unless Meeko stopped being a bitch and ran me my money I couldn't afford it. I had just enough left on my credit card to pay for one more month of tuition and that bitch would be maxed. But then, what would me and my children do for money? What would I do when that damn bill came in the mail? True enough I could have easily gone to my parents and got the money to knock that shit out, BUT I didn't want to go that route. I made this bed and didn't want to hear shit about nobody having to "bail me out" because I fell on my face. So, I went home and started working on my resume. I could always go back to school but right now I needed to get my grind on to take care of my responsibilities.

I was glad that Mikey's school was a block away and being that he was almost 9, I didn't have to be there to pick him up. I never thought my baby would be a latchkey kid but shit was, what it was. He would be able to walk home from school with his friends, go inside and start his homework until I or my dad got there. On most days, my dad would be home before him, but it was still days he was gonna have to be on his own for an hour or two. Mykia wouldn't have to be picked up until 6, so I was good til work until 5… 5:30 depending on what area I found a job in.

I started cooking dinner as I worked on my resume because I was planning to talk to my daddy about all this shit when he got in. I kinda hated that I was gonna need him to look out for Mikey on some days because again, my father was pissed about me getting pregnant with Mikey back then. So I already knew when he found out I was going to get a job because Meeko ass had hung me out to dry... He was gonna give me that "I told your dumb ass so" look over the rim of his glasses that I couldn't stand. I was mentally preparing myself for him and his condescending tone, and my mother and her pom-poms with Meeko name on them once she got wind of what was happening. I could hear her now hollering about I was overreacting to this whole situation with Meeko. She was too strung out on his Uncle Slim these days to see the monster Meeko had become. I knew in the coming weeks I was gonna smoke a WHOLE LOTTA WEED to cope with all the changes going on in my life as well as my parents and their opinions and shit.

That night I stuffed my dad full of Fried Chicken breast, rice with gravy, green beans with white potatoes, cornbread muffins and iced tea with lemon which was his favorite. He knew my ass wanted something the minute he walked through the door and those aromas from the kitchen hit his ass in the nose. Once the kids were in bed, I fixed him a big ass bowl of ice cream with a glazed donut on the side and took it to him while he was in his office. He was on the phone but got when I showed up and pretty quick I might add. I sat across from my dad and told him what I wanted to tell him about the shit that was going on in my life and although it killed me, I told him what I needed from him….. just to help out with Mikey some days depending on my hours. But I was determined to make it work. When I was done giving my spill, my daddy walked over and kissed me on my forehead and told me he was here in my corner and whatever I needed to get over this bump in my road he was here to help. I felt so relieved hearing that and glad he for once wasn't giving me a whole spill about how I had fucked up and if I had just listened to him. I still wasn't ready to talk to Malissa about it yet though.

For the next two weeks, things flowed kinda smoothly. The kids adjusted to their new schools fairly easily. Meeko hadn't bothered me and I hadn't bothered him. It kinda messed me up with Mikey would want to see him but couldn't. I didn't tell him why, just that he would call soon and to chill. Chico and I were growing closer. I finally invited him over to chill and watch movies with me once the kids were asleep. My dad came home during this time and the formal introduction was made. I was nervous, but it wasn't as bad as I was expecting. Chico was polite and respectable, and when my dad interrupted our movie time for a man to man with him... I don't know what was asked or said because neither of them would share with me what they talked about.... I just know Chico was like Rev cool as shit, which was a bold face lie cause Pastor Ike was everything BUT cool in my opinion. And the next morning at breakfast, my dad told me that Chico was alright in his book and was welcomed around anytime. I didn't know what the fuck that was supposed to mean and it had me eyeing them from the side because if it meant what I thought it was meaning they were gonna be in for a rude awakening.

Easter Weekend came around and I finally decided to introduce Chico to my children. I had waited for a number of reasons, mainly because although I was dating him, my babies didn't need a dad. They had a hell of a dad, they just couldn't see him right then. But being as though my dad had invited him to come for service on Easter Sunday and he gladly accepted, I figured now was the time. In the whole time I had known Meeko, he had never stepped foot in anybody church. Not that I was judging him for that because my ass was far from perfect, BUT being as though I was raised that a family that prays and worships together stays and prospers together it had me looking back on what we shared with different eyes. Like how could we really have ever had a successful marriage when we couldn't even come to God together. We had never prayed together or anything. Don't get me wrong, Chico agreeing to come to church so readily didn't have me looking at his ass with Wedding bells gleaming in my eyes or no shit like that. I couldn't say the same my father sadly, although I didn't see it off the break.

On Easter Sunday, he met us at church looking sharper than a set of ginsu knives. He was decked out in an all white Armani suit, which complimented the white BCBG dress I wore. We didn't plan it that way, it just worked out like that. My dad welcomed him with open arms. I mean Ike was grinning like the nigga was there chasing after his ass the way he was grinning from ear to ear, introducing him to folks and calling him son. Not only had Chico come to worship with us but he brought his mother, Miss Emma and his daughter Aaliyah. I was trying not to be bothered by this, so on the surface I kept it cute, but underneath I was kinda pissed.

I knew Chico was digging me deep and that was cool but during our conversations we had agreed that although I was his "girl" or whatever, we were taking shit slow. I was just really letting go of my first love. I had been wrapped up in this nigga for years, had kids and a whole life with him so while I was open to the prospect of us I needed time and space also. Meeting his mother and daughter were not on my list of things to do that weekend. However, they were there and I didn't want to be an ass so I sucked it up and made the most of it. I figured maybe it was just my fear of moving on and forward that had me being hypersensitive.

My mother and Vikki also came to church that morning. It had been awhile since Malissa had been in my father's church but they still respected her as the estranged First Lady that she was. Although I was happy to see my mother, I didn't say too much because we still hadn't spoke since she sided with Meeko in so many words and while we needed to address it, my Father's church on Easter Sunday with a packed house was NOT the place to address it. I laughed to myself when she texted me to tell me how I was making myself look bad running around with this new nigga when I aint even officially done with the old one. I texted her back and quickly reminded her that she was fucking Slim, Meeko's uncle, out of both pants legs and she was still MARRIED to my father. She aint want to deal with that shit though. So that was the last time we spoke until this day.

After church we all went to Michelle's for dinner including Chico and his family. Even my mother came. Michelle was so excited to entertain everyone, as well as show off her home and family. My mother was excited to finally meet her granddaughter, Michelle's two week old baby girl Heather. It was a joyous occasion for the most part. We even talked to Amber on the phone and Video chatted with Nikki since neither of them could make it. I did have to check Mikey again about his attitude. His little ass was throwing Chico maaaaad shade. I understood he was still in his feelings about Meeko, and finding out I had a "friend" all of a sudden probably added to his level of pisstivity, HOWEVER, under no circumstances was I going for the disrespect. Not because Chico was my man, but simply because he was an adult and Mikey ass knew better. I wanted to knock his ass out but being as though we were in someone else home with a house full of people I didn't want to embarrass him. So I called him upstairs and had a conversation with him. Once I let him know that if he didn't check his attitude I was gonna check his whole ass, he pulled it together. I mean he shut down all the way and just didn't say too much of nothing to anybody. I felt bad because I knew he was going through it with everything happening and changing so fast but I just couldn't let him get away with being disrespectful to ANY adult. Once he and I had a few minutes alone upstairs, he got his shit in order and we continued on with a nice Easter Dinner with family and new friends.

On Easter Monday, Chico and I took the

kids to the "Black Family Reunion at the National Zoo. I felt like it was too soon for "family outings" and shit, but Chico pulled my card by bringing it up at the dinner table in front of everybody. I wasn't gonna embarrass him in front of everybody and tell him hell no, so I agreed. Deep down inside I felt like he knew that too. Mikey was cool the whole day because I let him bring two of his good friends with him, so he was focused on them instead of the fact that mama got a man now. Chico had been trying hard with Mikey and his friends all day but they wasn't into him… until we left the zoo and he took us down to Fun Land in Fredericksburg. It was like a Chuck E Cheese, Dave & Busters and Amusement Park all rolled into one. Once the boys got there and Chico let them burn up his pockets willingly with Go Karts, Paddle Boats, Batting Cages, Bumper Cars, and Lazer Tag, all their little asses was team Chico.

We stayed and played until about 10pm then we grabbed some pizza and got a room. I had already called Mikey's homeboy's parents and got the OK to keep them overnight. We got a suite and kept it cute. Chico ass slept on the sofa because although I was glad Mikey was coming around with getting to know him and all, he would never see his mother laying in the bed with a man outside of his dad. That wasn't an image I planned on putting in my baby head at all.

The next day after checkout, we ended up stopping at Potomac Mills on the way back and Chico treated all the kids to fresh Jordan's. I though it was sweet that he made sure nobody was left out. I didn't say anything but it was clear that Chico now had a friend in Mikey, so much so he even rode back with him instead of me.

When we got back to the house, Mikey and his friends thanked Chico for their shoes and took off in the house. Chico and I chatted briefly and decided to head out to dinner together that night. I needed a little time to get the kids straight and get myself together, so we agreed he would pick me up at 7pm. I kissed him on the cheek and then went on in the house. When I walked in, my dad was sitting on the sofa in the living room listening to Mikey and his friends tell him about all the fun they had with "Mr. Chico". I could hear the pots and pans clicking and clanging in the kitchen and something was smelling hella good. I told my daddy he didn't have to have Michelle come all the way here to cook, I would've hooked something up. My daddy smile responded before he did when he told me Michelle wasn't there. Before I could even ask who was up in the kitchen making it smell like the night before Thanksgiving, the mystery chef emerged from the kitchen…

Sister Patterson.

I didn't understand why the fuck she was strutting around my mother's kitchen. As I looked her up and down trying to control my WHAT THE FUCK face that was on display, I realized that SIS was way too comfortable. She didn't have on any shoes, she had her hair pinned up and her face was fresh. She looked as though she had been there for a while. She smiled at me, but it took no time for that motherfucka to fade when she realized a smile was NOT something I had to share with her. I couldn't believe this shit."

     Ike looks over at Mikki who is offering his guest the stank face. His smile quickly transforms into a scowl because to him it is clear his youngest child has lost her mind. "Where are your manners Marissa? I know you see Betty standing there."

     "Betty Huh? I swore she was SISTER Patterson." Mikki snaps with and eye roll.

     Betty nervously chuckles. "It's okay, Betty is fine."

     "So what's this daddy?

     "What do you mean what's this?" Ike checks his tone realizing that Mikey and his friends are taking all of this conversation in. "Meet me in my office in five minutes and then we can discuss this." Ike gets up and walks over to Betty and kisses her on the cheek before leaving and heading downstairs to his home office.

     Mikki sits there with a disgusted look on her face

for a moment then she gets up.

"Mikki I….." Betty tries to explain.

"It's Marissa, feel free to call me Marissa. And I will continue to call you SISTER PATTERSON." Mikki stands up and picks up Mykia. "Come on y'all, lets go." Mikki walks out the door and the Mikey and his friends follow behind her.

"I was beyond pissed with this entire situation. My daddy knew better. I couldn't even get my head on straight because it was so much swirling through it. Like seriously. My parents were STILL MARRIED and with my father being a man of God, that was supposed to mean something. I knew my mother was out here living life but as me and my sisters had discussed before she was going through a phase. She went out on a limb because of my situation back then, and she got caught up. Now she was having a moment and soon it would all be over and she would go sit her ass back next to my daddy as the first lady of his church and his life. But Ike ass was tripping tryna sneak one in with this church bitch.

I hopped in the rental with my kids and we just went riding around for awhile. I had a lot on my head and heart. I know it may sound like I'm ungrateful, but I was truly hating where my life was right now. I was trying to make the best of this shit, but it was hard to do that giving all that was swirling around me. When me and the kids were out L.A with my sister, she made it clear that if I really wanted to leave her door would always be open and I was strongly considering it. True I had recently started this whole thing with Chico, but I didn't even care. He was cool and had potential to be the one, but I was just so all over this place at the moment, trading in the East Coast for the West was starting to sound like a good idea.

As much as I hated doing so, I kept my children out late because I knew my daddy and like an alarm clock, he started up and shut down at the same times daily. I just knew by coming in at 10:30pm, Ike would be held up in his room for his nightly reflection and meditation before he went to bed, most importantly, I expected SISTER PATTERSON to be gone on where the fuck she lived. Boy was I surprised when I walked in the house and they both were sitting in the living room on the sofa waiting on my ass. I had a brief flash back to the day I walked in to my parents sitting on the sofa together and our whole worlds changed. I felt it in my bones that tonight, whatever my daddy was waiting on that sofa to say to me was gonna be another world changing conversation.

"Is she asleep?" Ike asks, referring to Mykia who is on Mikki's hip with her head resting on her shoulder.

"Yes."

"Take them upstairs and put them to bed and then come back. We need to talk."

"Daddy listen...."

"No. I've spoken. Now do as I asked Marissa."

"I'm extremely tired and need to get them to bed, can't this wait until the morning." Mikki asks, glaring at Sister Patterson.

"If it could, I wouldn't be sitting here. Now you got 5 minutes Marissa. Please don't test me." Ike says with finality that alerts Mikki to the fact that he means business. Without another word spoken, Mikki goes up the stairs and puts her children to bed before returning downstairs to the couple sitting in the same spot waiting. She sits down in the chair across from them and lets out an exaggerated sigh. "Okay, I'm here."

"Marissa, I know you are going through a lot in your own life right now, and since the day you came back home, I have been supportive of you. I've respected the decisions you have made, even when I didn't agree. I've been your rock in the middle of this storm you are wading through...."

"Daddy I know all this..." Mikki interrupts with an attitude.

"I'm talking." Ike bellows, raising his voice an octave and silencing Mikki. "Now the way you behaved today was not only childish but trifling...

"Daddy....."

"Last time I'ma tell you I AM TALKING NOW." Ike grabs Betty's hand. "You owe Betty an apology immediately for the way you carried on today. Not simply because she's my woman but because I didn't raise you like that."

"Ike, it's okay. We did kinda spring this on her, so I

understand her being upset." Betty chimes in, trying to ease the tensed situation.

"I understand her being upset also. But what I don't understand, nor will I tolerate is her being disrespectful and she knows this. So again, Marissa, you own Betty an apology for your behavior today."

" I apologize for being rude as you say but I don't apologize for how I feel. All our lives we heard you preach about the sanctity of marriage, yet here you are all but forgetting about yours daddy and that's not right."

"What makes you think I've forgotten about my marriage Marissa? Let me remind you of something, I was very much happy and very much in love with my wife, your mother. But as I would think you would understand by now all the time happiness and love aint enough."

"How is that so? Love and Happiness is what marriage is made of Daddy."

"Marissa, excuse my language, but the shit you just said is why I thank God every day that you haven't gotten married yet. Baby girl, so much more goes into making a marriage work. Love and Happiness together only make up about 60% of the whole pie."

"I feel like this, you and mommy were happy until I got pregnant and that was a test we all failed as a family. Mommy got caught up and it wont be long before she is ready to come back home. You as her husband, and a man of God is supposed to be there waiting for her." Mikki explains her theory.

"Marissa, baby." Ike reaches over and grabs her hand and pulls her over to the sofa and has her sit between him and Betty. He gently wipes the tears that have started to fall from his youngest daughter eyes. "Mikki, there are days I reflect back on when your mother and I were raising you girls. A part of me hates how much we sheltered y'all from. Especially you and Nikki because you two were the babies of the bunch. Mikki, I love your mother. That woman will always own a piece of my heart. But baby girl, we stopped being compatible long before that day she took you and Nikki and ran off.

"What?" Mikki asks in shock.

"Mikki, your mother and I realized our marriage was over with before we even came to DC. We honestly tried, and we agreed to stay together until you girls were all out of the house. Your mother hated the thought of moving to DC, but we agreed to hold the family together for you girls so that's why we were still together. Then you got pregnant, I lost my mind and the end was here sooner than we anticipated."

"But Daddy, You and mommy…."

"Gave y'all and the world what yall needed to see. Now we are both at a place where we are ready to let it go. I've prayed about it, she's prayed about it. We've talked about it and everything and we decided that its time."

"I just don't know what to say."

"And I understand that baby. It's a lot to take in."

"So I have to ask, how long have y'all been seeing each other?"

"Marissa, I can assure you as long as your mother and I were together, even for a while after she left I was not with another woman."

Marissa turns and looks at Betty. "Sister Patterson, I'm trying. I really am. But it's hard knowing that you know my mother."

"You are right, and I understand that. Your mother and I have talked about this. When your father first asked me out, I told him I needed to talk to her first. We met up and sat down and had a loooong conversation. The only thing your mother asked of me was that I treat him right back then."

"Wait, so again how long have y'all been together."

"It's been close to 3 years now."

"So why now? Why now are y'all clueing us all in

to y'all relationship.

"Because Marissa, I've asked Betty to be my wife."

"Wow, this is…. Unbelievable."

"I know this is all new to you. So, I understand and I'm giving you space to process it all. My thing is this, while you don't have to love or like it…. You WILL respect it. The same way you demand respect of your children to your relationships, I'm demanding it of you to mine. Got me?"

"Yes daddy."

"I love you." Ike smiles at his daughter and pulls her into his loving embrace.

"I love you too daddy."

"Always?" Ike asks jokingly.

"Always." Mikki sits up and kisses him on the cheek. Mikki stands up. "Sister Patterson, I….."

"Before you say anything else, I have something I want to say. I know all of this is new to you, and I understand that you always have been and always will be Ike's baby. I'm never trying to take your dad away or replace your mother. I know it takes time to earn someone's love, I'm no fool. The same way it took time for me and Ike's love to grow, it will take time with you girls. All I'm asking for is a fair shot and that you don't shut me out because of what used to be. Is that fair?"

"Yes. That's fair."

Betty stands up and hugs Mikki. "And calling me Betty is just find Marissa."

"It's Mikki. Feel free to call me Mikki."

Ike stands up and hugs both of them and kisses them both on the cheek before giving thanks to God for guiding them to understanding. With that, they all head upstairs. Mikki goes into her room and closes the door while Ike and Betty go into the master bedroom and do the same.

"I laid awake for a while just thinking about the conversation I had with my daddy and my soon to be step mother. I had mixed feelings about all that was revealed, but it was his life at the end of the day, so I had to accept it. It was crazy how I had just gone through the same thing with my son. I wanted him to be respectful, so I had to model the same behavior I was demanding of him. I guess like all things, in time it would be okay one way or the other.

The next morning, Chico picked me up and we went to Breakfast. My daddy and Betty wanted to spend time with the kids because my daddy felt like the same way he had to explain this life move to me, he had to do the same with Mikey. Besides, I needed the break. After Breakfast, we rode up Chevy Chase and did a little shopping and finally snuck over to his house for a little afternoon delight. Chico dropped me off at home that night around 8:30. When I walked in, Betty and Mykia were chilling on the sofa watching cartoons, and my daddy and Mikey were on the floor playing connect four. My kids seemed to be taking to Betty with ease, so although it was still new to me I decided I was gonna take a page from their book and honor her request and give the woman a fair shot. I went upstairs and changed into some sweats and a T Shirt and came back down to hang out with them, that's when Betty told me she had messages for me.

Three of the places I had submitted my resume to had called. I was so excited and couldn't wait to return those calls the next morning.

The next Morning, I was up before the sun getting my mindset together for the day ahead of me. After I prayed, I made coffee and breakfast for all of us and around 9am, while Betty and the kids watched cartoons and my daddy was off to visit a parishioner that was in the hospital, I went downstairs to my daddy's office and started returning telephone calls. I was on the phone until about 11:30am and when I was done I had three interviews set up. Two for the next day which was Thursday and one for Friday.

I was so giddy I ran upstairs to share my news with Betty and the kids and she was genuinely happy for me. They all came upstairs to help me get my clothes together for the next day and I was so glad I had "church clothes" galore because I could easily put some interview shit together. While I was changing purses, I found an envelope at the bottom with 5,000 dollars in it from Chico. I couldn't do nothing but smile because he was definitely shooting his shot. And I'd be lying if I said I didn't like it. True it was some shit I wasn't feeling, but for the most part I could see Chico was genuinely a good dude and well I deserved that. As long as he took heed to what I said to him about taking it slow and respecting that this was all new to me as I was coming off of something both painful and long term and I needed time… we would be good.

I called him to thank him for my little surprise. I wouldn't accept money from him flat out so I thought it was sweet that he surprised me with it cause I'd be lying my ass off if I said I didn't need it. True I could've asked my parents for it, but I was a grown ass woman and had gotten myself into the situation and was determined to climb out of it on my own. Chico kept acting like he had no idea what I was talking about which was cute. Since I was in such a good mood, I invited him over for dinner that evening with us.

I left Mykia in the house with Betty having her read the same books over and over again to her while Mikey went to the playground with his friends and I went to the Safeway to get the stuff I needed for dinner. Alana called and asked me to come down but I told her I had dinner guest coming etc and went on and took my ass in the house. I had a serious day to get ready for the next day so beating the block would have to wait.

I got back home and hung out with Betty and my daughter while I cooked Spaghetti with ground turkey, salad and garlic bread. I brought a Sock-It-To-Me cake from the grocery store because I aint have time to do all that. Like seriously baking cakes and shit on a Wednesday was so not my forte.

As usual Chico was on time. At 6:30 he showed up ready for dinner and even brought a bottle of wine with him to go with dinner. My dad was damn near more giddy than I was when he opened the door and he was standing there. I really don't know why, but it really bothered me deep inside when I saw my daddy get all giddy over Chico, calling him son and shit. It always made me think about how he never gave Meeko a chance. Shit was doomed from jump. I tried not to dwell on it, but I swear every time I saw them together my mind immediately went to that. I'm not even sure why I gave a fuck about it because well as you know Meeko and I were DONE.

Although my mind was preoccupied with the shit that had gone down with Meeko, I enjoyed dinner for the most part. By 9pm, we were all in the living room standing in prayer as my daddy prayed for me that my potential be seen by those it needed to be seen by on my series of interviews and that God order my steps to what was meant for me. With an Amen, we all said good night to Chico and I hurried to finish getting myself together for the next day.

Interview day!

I was nervous as hell from the moment I woke up because well I hadn't had a job since I was in high school. That was at a shoe store and was just to appease my mother, so it had no bearing on my future. Now here I was a grown woman with two small children I needed to really get out on my own and build a life for. So, I needed this.

My first interview was for a Senior Data Entry Person at a Real Estate Law Firm. Being as though I had an actual real estate license and a padded resume I was told I had been pulled to the top of the pile. My father had a whole church so of course I put that I worked there for three solid years as the office manager. I put Vikki down as my contact person because well, while I knew Pastor Ike wanted me to get the Job I wanted he wasn't gonna lie for me to help me get it. The interview went okay I guess. It didn't feel like the place for me though. The interviewer told me they would be making their decision by the close of business Friday and would be in touch.

I left and went on my second interview which was for an entry level loan officer with a small mortgage company. It too went okay, however I wasn't impressed with the thought of working on weekends being as though I had two small children I needed to make time for. I also wasn't too impressed with the salary. Again, I had two small children so working for peanuts wasn't on my list of shit to do ya know. They offered me the job on the spot and while I was flattered I asked for a day or two to think it over. I explained I was a single mom and while I had my family support I needed to talk to them to make sure they would be able to back me up with things like watching the children when I had to work weekends etc. The supervisor didn't seem happy that I didn't jump at the opportunity and left me with "That's fine." Then went on to tell me that by me not taking the job immediately that they were going to continue with their interviews scheduled for today... and if they happen to come across another viable candidate who is ready then they would move forward with them. I knew then that wasn't the place for me because I could already see they didn't give a shit about their employees' personal obligations. It was about their bottom line and while I needed this job, my children would ALWAYS come first.

I went home and prayed for a better outcome on the next day.

On Friday morning I got up and prayed with my daddy before jetting off to my third and final interview. This was the job I actually wanted of all three. It was for an Assistant Project Manager with an interior design company based in Rockville, Maryland. The interviewer was impressed with me. I knew my shit due my degree in interior design and my portfolio of the work I had done on Meeko's club spoke for itself. I was also impressed with the company and the position. The starting salary was 65,000 a year with full benefits from day one of my contract. I would get my own office. Two weeks paid vacation after six months and a 2500 dollar signing bonus. This was where I wanted to be!

My interview ended up lasting longer than expected. A LOT longer to be exact. The president of the company loved my enthusiasm and decided to cut to the chase and gave me what he liked to call the test of all test. He had me walk him through a design for an apartment in Beverly Hills. The whole thing was computer generated from the specks to the budget and I showed my ass! I brought my design in under budget and it was impressive. I wasn't afraid or nervous and talked to him the whole time about the hows and whys and even when he verbally threw curve balls in at me, I was on it. I was in my element and he said he could see my passion already. His next question was when could I start and he told me I had better say MONDAY!

I was so excited I damn near jumped in his arms and hugged him. I wanted to start Monday but I still had other obligations and I didn't want *to jump in over my head so I told him as soon as I finished my Finals in May. I explained that I was currently finishing up my Business degree and while I would love to start immediately, I wouldn't be able to because I was scheduled to graduate in June. I explained that I wanted to walk through the door ready to give my all and be 110% in. I got so nervous when he told me not to worry because I just knew he was gonna withdraw the offer, but then he smiled.*

He told me he was glad I had my priorities in order and was gonna talk to his partners and PUSH FOR ME because this was a position they wanted to fill immediately, but he wanted to fill it with ME. I thanked him and left. I was so worried that I got in the car and prayed and cried. I wanted and NEEDED this opportunity for myself and my children, but I needed to finish school also. I really hoped they could see where I was coming from because I would be crushed if they went with somebody else. As soon as I said Amen, my phone rung and it was Mr. Lewinski. I was damn near holding my breath as he spoke because that was FAST and I just knew his partners said tell that bitch to reapply when she gets her life in order…. We need somebody NOW.

Mr. Lewinski said they had agreed to let me finish school and I would start July 6th. He had a project coming up that I would be perfect for….

As the LEAD. I was so happy I literally screamed in his ear and the tears just started flowing. He told me he would send me an email with my official offer letter etc and would see me on the 6th of July. I couldn't thank him enough!

I floated all the way home to share my news with my family. My daddy was so proud of me. On Saturday, Chico took us all out to celebrate. I had been on a high all weekend since nailing my start in my career field on Friday then Monday rolled around and I had to look at Meeko as in court.

We had our hearing for my protective order and it was ugly. The judge opted to clear the court due to the nature of the evidence that had been presented. Listening to Meeko threatening my life once again hurt so bad. I couldn't for the life of me understand 1) Why the fuck I loved him so much despite how he treated me constantly and 2) Why he treated me so fucked up despite how much I loved his trifling ass.

I looked over at Meeko with tears that had a mind of their own falling without my permission as he stood next to his high-priced lawyer he opted to hire for this shit. Lucky for me, his high-priced attorney had no standing with the female judge who you could tell as hard as she tried to be indifferent about the shit was the fuck over men like him and their bullshit.

The judge quickly granted my motion for an order of protection. The order was to last 90 days and would be revisited when we went back to family court being as though we had children that he had a right to visit unless that judge saw fit to keep it in standing. Meeko, immediately got pissed and did what Meeko did best… show his entire ass. He went off and started screaming about how I was being a bitch and was keeping him from his kids. I was about to speak but the judge interjected and told him from the shit she heard on the tapes it sounded like it was the other way around… HE was the parent that was using the children as pawns in our break up, and again ultimately the judge in family court would decide if and when he could see them but for now he needed to respect the order and STAY AWAY FROM US.

Two weeks later we had our appearance in Family Court. Again, he had his lawyer there and when he saw we had yet another female judge, he was pissed. I didn't get an attorney although people in my circle had suggested that I should because he had one. I felt it was a waste of money because I felt that no over-priced attorney could tell my story to the judge better than I could.

Child support was entered in my favor for

both children totaling 1500.00 dollars per month. The judge ordered back payment for Mikey going back three years and for Mykia from the day she was born since that was around the time we could agree that the relationship dissolved. I wasn't expecting the whole arrearage thing to come about at all. Once it all was tallied Meeko was ordered to pay me a total of 45,000 dollars in back child support. 27,000 for Mikey and 18,000 for Mykia. You could see the smoke coming out of his fucking ears. I just kept thinking if he had just given me my fucking money out of his basement when he threw my shit out on the lawn, I would've NEVER even gone through with all this. So I didn't give a fuck about him being mad. Just give me my goddamn money!

The judge continued on and it was my turn to be pissed. The judge entered an order of full joint custody which meant he had just as much right when it came to making decisions regarding our children as I did. The judge also honored his request and the time with the children was split 50/50. I had them two weeks per month and he had them the other two. Holidays were spent with whoever time it was with them. I was LIVID.

The order of protection was amended and no longer included my children... just me. We had to agree on a neutral party that I was required to drop the kids off at before 8pm on the *day his time with the children started and he was to return them by the same time on the day mine started. He was still supposed to stay 200 feet away from me and could not contact me in any manner. I put my dad down as the person he needed to contact in the event of an emergency and he put Inda down for his. We walked out the courtroom both pissed because in a sense the judge had cut the baby down the middle. I got my money, but had to give up a whole two weeks with my fucking kids every month and it was gonna take me some time to wrap my mind around that shit. I never thought things would ever become this fucked up between Meeko and I, yet here we were.*

A week after our court hearing I got a call from Meeko's attorney. He informed me he had a check for me and I could come to his office and pick it up. Once I got out of school I picked up Mykia and we headed downtown to pick up the check. It was in the amount of 30,000. I signed for it, thanked him and left with a HUGE smile on my face. The next morning, which was Saturday, I was at the bank when the doors to that bitch opened. I opened a checking and a savings account for me and put 5 grand in each one. I opened 3 high interest CD for myself and my kids. I put 5,000 in each and the final 5 grand I took in cash.

My daddy and I went to the dealership and I used 1500 dollars as I down payment on a brand new Dodge Magnum. I took another 1500 and took my kids shopping and used a grand to pay off my credit card bill. That Monday while the kids were in school, I went apartment hunting. I was graduating in two weeks and started my new job soon. It was time I had my own space. Besides that, I had a boyfriend that well I wanted to spend time with also. I had never laid up with a man in my Daddy's house outside of Meeko and I wasn't about to try and make a habit of that, so I needed my own and went to find it.

I went and saw a few spots filled out some applications, paid some fees and by Wednesday, I started getting calls. I ended up taking a 3 bedroom in Oxon Hill, Maryland. It was spacious as hell and had two full bathrooms and a den. I couldn't wait to sign my damn lease and finally for once have something that was truly mine. I had lived alone before but never truly had my own until now. I was finally realizing what being a woman consisted of. On Thursday morning, I dropped the kids off at school and went and got two money orders from the post office and headed out to sign my lease. I was so excited I couldn't stop smiling. I signed my lease and grabbed my keys but wasn't gonna start staying there just yet.

That night me and my daddy went for a walk together, just me and him and I told him I was moving out. He was so scared that I was about to make the mistake and move in with Chico, that's when I proudly produced my lease and showed it to him that had my name as the leaseholder and my children as the occupants. I knew he liked Chico, but he was never gonna like any man who wanted me to suck his dick, wash his drawls and fry his chicken without handing me his last name to wear proudly as I preformed those said duties. So he was proud of me. I was finally getting my grown woman on. I could kinda see him battling with the double edge sword because on one hand he was proud of me for finally coming into my own. I mean we all know how I went off on my own solo fuck up your life tour for quite some time. But here I was now, finally with some shit in my own name that I was working for on my own. I was about to graduate COLLEGE and walk right into my career. True I was a few years off due to choices I made in the past, but that was neither here nor there. All that matter was the place I was standing in now. So while he was proud of me, he also didn't want me to go.

He wouldn't come right out and say it, but I knew the time that had been lost between my dad and I bothered him. I don't know if it was the guilt of trying to have me burned at the stake for getting pregnant with Mikey or just the time he missed out on with us, but he loved having us home. He tried to put if off on Betty about how she was gonna be sad I was taking them babies from her. And while I know on some surface she would be because in the short amount of time we had all been in the same space she had come to absolutely adore my babies and they felt the same way. Mikey started calling her G-Ma Bee and she was so excited. She ate that shit right on up and baked his greedy ass some chocolate chip cookies from scratch. And I would be lying if I said she wasn't growing on me. I loved seeing my daddy happy and she was helping to bring that happiness about. And it was nice to see my children with a TRADITIONAL grandma FINALLY! Don't get me wrong, I loved my mother with all my heart and Inda as well BUT they both was still out here in these streets so to speak. It wasn't uncommon to find their asses at the club on a weekend, or running off on girls trips or too busy playing with dick to play with their grandkids. Now they loved them without question and would give them the world but don't you DARE ask them to babysit. Inda would tell you quick BABYSIT MY ASS! You better call a cousin, niece, nephew or something. So it was nice that now they had a bonus grandma that was the polar opposite of the other two aka Frick and Frack and all she wanted to do was love up on them.

When the weekend rolled around, I spent it with Chico in a sense. He was helping me get my apartment together before we officially went home. I had spent the week putting together a layout of what I wanted and how I wanted shit to be from the colors to the drapes and all. So on Saturday while the apartment was being painted, Chico and I went furniture shopping. He paid for the painters claiming it was a "box warming gift" to me. It wasn't a house so we didn't call it that. When we went furniture shopping I knew he was coming with the bullshit because he kept insisting on paying for the furniture. I declined each and every time and used what I had to take care of that. When we stopped to eat lunch that's when he came with the conversation that had been looming over us since the day I dangled my keys in his face.

"So you think the kids gonna like the new place?" Chico asks before taking a huge bite of his burger.

"I believe they will. They each got their own rooms that's gonna reflect them. Only thing Mikey probably be pissed about is moving away from his friends. Granted he will still see them daily but you know how kids are."

"Yeah that's true. So what about you, you excited?"

"Yes lawd! I cannot wait! I love my daddy and Bee but I swear to GAWD I can't wait to be in my own space."

"Your big headed ass could've been in your own space Mikki. I been told you to come and stay with me."

"I know Chico. You did tell me that."

"The kids would've had to share a room for a second, but my lease is up next month anyway and we could've got a house or some shit boo."

"Yeah." Mikki says just to fill the space with a response.

"But since you done went and got another box and shit. You got a year lease too right?"

"You know it's a year Chico."

"So you think we gonna be ready to get that house when your lease is up?"

"I don't know Chico. Let's just see where this year takes us." Mikki smiles at him trying to soften the blow.

"Well I already know where I want the year to take us. To the alter."

"Is that right?" Mikki laughs.

"What's funny Mikki?"

"Nothing Chico. It wasn't a funny laugh. Goodness. It was a in shocked laugh because that's not something we have discussed."

"It don't have to be discussed until after I put that ring on your finger."

"That's not how it works at all."

"Mikki I want you as my wife and the only people I need to have a discussion with before I come to you with a ring is God and your Father?"

"Wow, so what I feel and think and if I'm ready for all that don't even matter huh?" Mikki asks annoyed. "You know what, let's just drop this conversation Chico because it's about to change courses and a weekend that is supposed to be beautiful is about to switch courses."

"Why because I'm telling you I love you and want to Marry you."

"Chico we aint even been messing with each other that long to be talking Marriage and shit."

"Oh but you was okay talking marriage with that nigga Meeko tho."

"Whoa!" Mikki wipes her mouth with her napkin and pushes her food away. "You can get the check because this lunch is over. What went on between Meeko and I had nothing to do with you and I can't even understand why you bringing that man up. He don't bring up my relationship with you AT ALL."

"Because I doubt you have even told him you are in a relationship with me. Have you?"

"I didn't know I was supposed to considering me and him don't speak AT ALL. Legally CANT SPEAK! And I really do not fucking appreciate you stepping over all kinds of lines with this conversation. Our relationship is our relationship just like my relationship with him back then was between he and I. Now get the check I'm ready to go!" Mikki stands up to leave.

Chico stands up and grabs her hand. "Mikki wait. Sit down. Look I apologize. It's just…. Look can you sit down so we can talk."

"Pay the check and we can talk in the car. I'm ready to go." Mikki yanks away from him and walks outside the restaurant. Chico goes in his pocket and pulls out a crisp 100 dollar bill and throws it on the table then signals for the waiter, letting him know to keep the change and then runs out after Mikki.

"I stood at Chico's truck with a scowl on my face that could've killed him dead if looks were truly lethal. Like where the fuck did he really think he got off coming at me like that? He

came and opened my door for me and I climbed in and sat back with nothing to say. I was really in my feelings about the way he threw what I had been through with Meeko up in my face and it made me look at him different.

We rode back to my apartment where my car was parked at in total silence. I was hoping that he took the hint that I wasn't feeling his ass and went on about his business, but of course he didn't and before my feet hit the ground good he was out the truck and following me up the walkway. I started to turn around and bolt for my car and just leave, but I did want to see the job the painters did just to make sure everything was on the up and up.

When we got inside Chico and I kinda went off in different directions. He went to check the kitchen and bathroom while I went to scope out the bedrooms and den. I was standing in the den visualizing how everything would look once my furniture was delivered when Chico came up behind me and wrapped his arms around my waist.

"So you really mad with me now huh?" Chico asks and lovingly kisses Mikki on her cheek.

"Yes Chico, I am."

"Why Mikki? That's what I don't understand. You

mad at me for loving you? That's crazy as fuck and you know it."

"First I didn't say that so please don't put words in my mouth. I'm mad because you went really low today to even bring up the shit with Meeko."

"I apologize boo. I will admit I was outta line, but that shit hurt when I'm telling you I wanna marry your big head ass and you telling me all this other crazy shit when you were ready willing and able to marry a nigga who didn't deserve you at all."

"And you don't think that maybe, just maybe that's why I wanna take shit slow now Chico. You right, I was ready willing and able to marry a nigga who meant me no good whatsoever. Me and you been fucking with each other how long? And already you hollering about Marriage and shit so yes its giving me pause and yes I do want to wait to make sure that when I go skipping off to be somebody goddamn wife, that they truly are for me!"

"So you can't see that I'm for you Mikki?"

"Chico again, this is the fucking beginning. We started kicking it in March and here it is June and you talking marriage. Everybody is for everybody in the beginning. Lets see if you still for me a year from now and then we can talk about all that you talking about. I think that's more than fair."

"When you say all that I'm talking about what you mean Mikki? Be specific."

"Living together, marriage and all that."

"Wait. What?" Chico asks in confusion taking a step back from Mikki. "So you telling me that you want to wait a whole year before we even live together?"

"Yes Chico. What you thought you was about to move in Monday too?"

"Not Monday but I was thinking when my lease is up next month. It only makes sense."

"Well apparently you and I have been riding two

different waves because Chico just keeping it real with you, us living together is not something I'm trying to do right now."

"And why not? I'm really not understanding you right now."

"Because. This is MY first apartment. True I've been from under my parents roof more than once but that was always Meeko shit. This is finally mine. I need to experience what it's like to be on my own, handling my own shit for me and my kids before I start talking about playing house and shit again."

"You are fucking unbelieveable."

"No you are because I can't believe you giving me all this fucking grief when you already knew how I felt. I have two motherfucking kids who whole world just got turned upside down with me and their father splitting up. I need time before I have them looking at another motherfucking man walking around in his drawls drinking up all the motherfucking orange juice! RESPECT THAT!"

"You sound dumb as shit Mikki because I'm willing to bet you every motherfucking dollar I have saved that his ass done moved on and its another bitch up in his house, baking biscuits and shit and she gonna still be there doing it while your fucking kids there!"

"I don't give a fuck who or what the fuck he has going on at his house Chico! This is about me and mine and again you can respect my decision, or you can get the fuck on!"

"Daaaaamnnn." Chico looks at Mikki in shock. He chuckles in an attempt to hide his hurt. "Good to know how you really feel."

"Chico listen…." Mikki begins to try to clear things up between them realizing she may have come off kinda harsh. She grabs his hand and he pulls away.

" Nah. It's cool. You right and I respect your decision."

"Chico…"

"So look, you good right? I'ma go ahead and get up outta here. I got some shit to take care of."

"Yeah I'm good. I'ma go now too. The kids leaving for their first two weeks with Meeko tomorrow so I wanna spend some time with them anyway."

"Alright bet. Call me when you got time."

"I will."

"I stood there and waited for the kiss that never came and I knew he was really hurt. He simply turned around and walked out the door leaving me standing in the middle of my empty space all alone.

Going through the bullshit with Chico gave me a major headache. I didn't feel like I was being unreasonable at all. Again, we had only been together 3 months and he was talking about splitting the rent and jumping the broom. I did like Chico and while I was a lot of places with him, being his live- in ass or his wife was not either place.

I waited about 30 minutes, just sitting in my empty space lost in my own thoughts. If somebody had told me back when Meeko was in my living room threatening to kill my whole father for trying to tear our little family apart by forcing me to kill our baby that this is how shit would end up between us, I would've bet the whole motherfucking farm that you were crazy. I swore Meeko loved my ass back then. I had no clue the nigga was just playing a role.

I finally left and went to go and spend time with my babies. Again, they were gonna be gone for two whole weeks. While we would talk on the phone that shit was nothing compared to being able to wrap my arms around my babies and kiss them goodnight. My heart was hurting just thinking about the bullshit. And it didn't help that the shit Chico had just thrown in my face about what Meeko was doing at his house with his bitch had me feeling shit all up in my chest. It was hard but I pushed it to the side because I was finally understanding that I could only control what I did in this life and the way I reacted to other people. As much as it hurt I couldn't make Meeko see the way he hurt me over and over and over again. I could only control how I responded to the fact that he couldn't see or didn't care how he constantly hurt me. Just like I couldn't control Chico and his push and want to get married and lived together. I could only control how I reacted to the shit. So with that, I went and picked up pizza and wings and went to my Dad's house for some mommy & me time with my kids.

While my dad and Betty were home, they knew that I needed space and time with just my babies and I started to take them to a hotel for a sleepover to make it special but we went on and stayed in. We ate pizza in bed, watched movies and played video games. The next morning we went to church as a family and I was surprised and both annoyed when Chico walked in and slid in the pew behind me. My dad lit up when he saw him slide in and only because I was in the house of the lord I didn't completely spaz out on his ass. I told him way beforehand that I wanted to spend time with my kids alone because this whole transition was new to us. It was the first time we had to go to through this. He said he understood, and I really thought he would chill considering how shit went down between us the day before. Yet here he was. I felt so disrespected and made a mental note to check his ass on that shit later because it wasn't cool and if we were gonna stand any kind of chance he needed to respect my space and my children and call me crazy but right then, hearing that nigga behind me singing hymns and shit felt so disrespectful to everything I stood for. I waited until my dad did the alter call and grabbed my kids giving the impression that we were going to the bathroom and sadly we rolled out the back door.

We went back to my dad's house and finished packing them up for their two week hiatus and once we changed clothes we went to the park. Chico called me what felt like every 20 minutes but I ignored his ass. I had told him I would see him Monday and now I didn't want to see his ass at all. After our time at the park, I took them to dinner at Fudds in the City down in Chinatown and finally, reluctantly headed towards Inda's house.

When we got there, Inda was sitting in the living room watching TV. I was hoping to drop the kids off without incident but when I stepped into the living room, the look on her face let me know she had some shit on her chest and she wouldn't be Inda if she didn't get that shit off. I kissed the kids, made them promise to be good and then was turning on my heels to make a mad dash for the door when she finally spoke up.

"Hold on Mikki, I wanna talk to you before you go."

"Inda I…." Mikki tries to wiggle out of the inevitable.

"Inda huh?" Inda chuckles at Mikki addressing her by her first name. It's been Ma for the past nine years so exactly when did that change?"

"I'm sorry. I just figured with everything going on between me and Meeko that …"

"Well see that's your problem. You trying to figure shit when this aint math Marissa, its family. Now come on and sit down because I want to talk to you. It will only take a minute." Mikki goes and sits down on the sofa opposite where Inda is sitting. "Mikey, take your sister upstairs and watch TV until your daddy get here baby."

"Ooooh Ma you in trouble." Mikey teases, causing both Mikki and Inda to laugh as he collects Mykia and heads upstairs.

Inda pats the spot next to her letting Mikki know to come and sit there. Once Mikki sits down beside her. Inda grabs her hand and lets out a deep sigh. "It's been a looong time since we had one of these talks."

"I know." Mikki agrees. "And I know what you gonna say too."

"You do? Then tell me. I'm all ears." Inda sits back to hear Mikki's rendition of how their conversation is about to go.

"Let me see ... You're upset with me that I took Meeko to court and now..."

"No." Inda interrupts. "I'm upset with both of y'all. This here situation is all bullshit and you both know it. This is not a way for those babies to be raised, being shuffled back and forth between y'all bullshit. Can't even see mommy and daddy in the same room at the same time because of a raggedy ass piece of paper. Y'all both know y'all wrong."

"That was his fault Inda! He jumped on me!"

"So you were innocent in that whole fiasco Mikki? You beat the hell out of that girl for absolutely nothing."

"For nothing? Wow! Really?"

"Just hear me out. Meeko loves you Mikki. Y'all been together for nine damn years and you should know by now aint a woman on this earth that can take your place in that boy heart and life."

"Correction, we have KNOWN each other for over nine years now. But truthfully speaking how long were we actually together? There was always some other bitch hiding in the shadows of our so-called relationship. If not that, then he was down south, or I was down south, or his ass was locked up and ..."

"Let's not forget WHY he was locked up Mikki!" Inda snaps to get Mikki off her high horse causing her to sit quietly looking down at the floor. "But that shit is neither here nor there. I know my son and I know where he wants to be and believe it or not, that's with you Mikki."

"He sure has a strange way of showing it. This nigga left me alone on Valentine's Day, a day you are SUPPOSED to be with the person you love so he could go and lay up with this chick. That shit hurt Ma." Mikki wipes away the tears that are welling up in her eyes. "And then that night I went to the house, the same bitch I left because of is there with him. He jumped on me and embarrassed me to protect her, and I'm supposed to believe that this is where his heart is right?" Mikki chuckles at how stupid Inda truly sounds.

Inda hugs Mikki as Mikki continues to wipe away tears. "I understand what you are saying Mikki. Both of y'all need to grow up, sit down and talk like two adults. Y'all done got way too old for all this fighting and beefing and carrying on. And now y'all got two babies y'all dragging through all this shit and it's not fair to them at all. Have y'all even thought about what this shit is doing to them?"

Just then, Meeko walks in the house talking on his cellphone. He stops dead in his tracks when he sees Mikki sitting there wrapped in his mother's arms, apparently crying. "Aye, let me hit you back right quick." Meeko hangs up and sticks his phone in his pocket. Mikki sits up and looks at him through red teary eyes. Neither of them speaks for a minute, just stare at each other, each in their own thoughts and feelings about where and what their relationship has come to. "I'ma wait outside Ma." Meeko breaks the silent standoff. "The restraining order says I can't be within 200 feet of her so once she leaves I'll come back."

"Shut the hell up boy!" Inda snaps. "I don't give a

shit what no damn order says. This is my goddamn house and that shit don't apply here."

"That shit sound good ma, but it actually does and since she like running to the police and shit now, I'm not about to get myself jammed up being in the same space as her."

"Michael Angelo I swear I'm not on your shit today either. Now sit down because we got some talking to do cause this shit aint right!"

"Ma I already told you …" Mikki begins to protest as she stands up to leave.

"Shut up and sit your ass down Mikki! Now don't think because you been running around here smelling yourself that I wont get in your ass little girl cause I will! Not sit down and shut up! Aint shit changed with me but the color of my hair child!"

Meeko sits down on the sofa across from his mother and his ex, who has also sat back down. "What's up ma? What you need to talk about so bad because this shit here is done."

"I just want to know when is all this crazy shit gonna end and things can get back to normal. Even if y'all decide not to be together anymore, this shit happening right now is not right and it's hurtful and unfair to those babies upstairs that didn't ask to be caught up in the middle of no bullshit."

"Ma, it's not me." Meeko chuckles. "This shit is all her doing and everybody know that. She done sat around, being weak minded and let her little friends get her all hyped up to run down to the courts with this shit. Even her own fucking mother said she wrong as fuck for how she carrying shit"

"No you did this when you put your hands on me! Threatened to kill me and then hid my fucking kids from me! So fuck what my own mother got to say about how I chose to handle my shit!"

"You sound dumb as fuck right now. How many times have I threatened your dizzy ass. I threaten you 65 motherfucking times a day and you aint dead yet. And you knew I was gonna give the kids back so stop being fucking dramatic."

"Fuck all that. Then you gonna jump on me for some white fucking whore bitch!"

"I didn't jump on you first of all. There you go being dramatic again. I choked you out because you wouldn't calm the fuck down. You had already beat the shit out the girl, putting on a whole fucking show for the whole neighborhood. Not only embarrassing the fuck out of yourself but embarrassing me too!"

"Fuck your embarrassment Meeko! How embarrassed you think I felt when I walked in the club that night and you sitting up there loving up on that bitch! Sitting there trying to explain shit to her like fuck me and my heart that you just broke! Like she fucking mattered and I didn't! Nigga fuck your embarrassment! You lucky I didn't kill that bitch!!" Mikki fires off on Meeko telling him how she really felt.

"Oh and your goofy ass would've been sitting right in a cell looking dumb as shit. The bitch father is a cop Mikki and all she had to do was call him as she was trying to day and …"

"SO WHAT!" Mikki jumps up with tears rolling down her face. "FUCK HER FATHER! FUCK HER TOO! YOU HURT ME AND I DIDN'T DESERVE THAT!"

"Mikki calm down." Inda stands up and lovingly rubs her back.

"I'm sorry ma but he making it seem like I'm supposed to care about his bitch or who in her corner."

"See what I mean Ma. She too fucking stubborn to even listen when you try and tell her dumb ass something for her own good."

"Okay both of y'all just calm down. Both of y'all take a

deep breath and lets start over." Inda ease Mikki back to sitting down on the sofa and she sits beside her and continues to rub her back lovingly. "Now Meeko, why are you so angry with Mikki? Talk to her. She's here and she is listening."

"Look ma, no disrespect, but I aint come here for all this. I just came to get my kids for my two weeks with them and then we out."

"No you not Meeko!" Inda snaps out. "Both of yall being ridiculous and acting like fucking fools dragging those kids through all this shit for nothing at all and I'm tired of it! This aint no way for them babies to live and y'all fucking know it!"

"Like I said, that's her. She the one who ran down to the court building and put a nigga on child support even though I been taking care of her ass and BOTH my fucking kids before they were even fucking born! Now her ho ass riding around in fucking brand new cars and shit like a nigga can't see whats really real." Meeko chuckles at the situation and shakes his head in pity as he gets up and heads upstairs to where his children are.

Mikki stands up and wipes her face. "Just tell that trifling bastard to be sure to have my fucking kids back here on time" Mikki walks out the front door slamming it so hard it bounces back open. She walks down to her car and gets in and speeds off.

"I was 23.8 levels passed pissed with this whole situation. The nerve of this nigga to act like he had done right by me the entire time we were so called together. Like negro do I really need to run down the slew of bitches you done did me dirty for? And I'm just talking about the ones

I knew about and could prove. Only God and Meeko trifling ass knew how many bitches he could apply "No Face, No Case" rules to because I had not a clue about who they were. Through it all, I realized I was more mad with myself than anyone. I was the dummy that hung around constantly waiting for a tiger to change its stripes. I was also mad as fuck with myself because I knew Meeko well, and I knew he was pleased as punch that he was still able to get under my skin. He thrived off this shit and it was a clear sign that I still cared. It was his way of knowing that I still loved him. People always think that the opposite of love is hate, when it's not. It's actually indifference. I wanted to be indifferent to Meeko and his bullshit so bad, but him being able to get me to explode and fall apart and display anger and hatred was just another sign that I loved him. And as long as Meeko knew I still loved him, he was gonna continue to be the arrogant asshole that he had become. Maybe he had always been that way but my love for him blinded me from really seeing it. I don't know. All I know is I was extremely tired of the shit altogether.

I went back to my daddy's house and went straight to bed. Okay not really. I got ready for bed, I got in bed, but all I could really do was cry because shit wasn't supposed to be like this. Chico called me 6 different times and I ignored his ass each time. I was over men and their bullshit and just wanted to be left the fuck alone.

I went through damn near two weeks of avoiding the world in so many words. I just wanted to be alone and get my head together and wrap my mind around my new reality. I went to my house one day, which was the day they delivered my furniture. I had planned to stay there, but then I felt so alone. I had lost the love of my life, my kids were gone and it was just me. Chico kept calling but I would just shoot him a text every now and again and let him know I was taking some time for myself. I finally woke up three days before my kids were scheduled to come home and decided to just accept shit for what it was. This was my reality now and I couldn't hide from it locked away in my old bedroom eating ice cream and crying. I had talked to Alana the day before and she agreed to help me take me and the kids clothes over to my spot and get it together, go grocery shopping and shit. Not that I really needed help for these little task, I just needed a little company. I hadn't kicked it with my folks in what felt like forever, so we were having us a girls day and getting my house and life back in order.

After my shower I threw on a pair of leggings and a shirt and my Jordan's and was out the door. I wanted to get an early start on my day because Alana and I were talking about going clubbing that night with some of the girls. I drove down to her house and went and kicked on the door, only to find myself in shock when Eric opened it … in his damn boxers. I just laughed and pushed passed him to go find her ass, and I did … in the kitchen cooking this nigga toast and eggs. I sat down at the table and laughed her ass out while she tried to ignore the fact that I caught her ass. She couldn't stop blushing if her life depended on it. I knew it wouldn't be long before he worked his way back into her good graces and his side of the bed. They had been together forever. Like since we were kids. So I knew eventually they would find a way to work their shit out. Meeko and I were the complete oppsite. And besides, Meeko and I didn't have what they did. A whole marriage licence.

After some small talk over breakfast, Alana told me to give her 20 minutes to shower and get herself together. I let her know I would be right back, I was gonna run and get gas and come right back. Eric asked if we wanted help but I declined. I didn't need him reporting back to his boy where I lived. I was sure he would wait until the kids were doing their two weeks with him and his bitch and firebomb my fucking spot.

I drove to the gas station around the corner and was minding my business letting my gas pump while I grabbed me a Pepsi, 2 blunts, some salt & vinegar chips and a hot sausage from the mini mart. Once I got my munchies food because I was definitely gonna put something in the air, I was waiting patiently for the tank to fill up when MY Escalade pulled up at the next pump over, blasting Rare Essence early in the morning. I didn't know what today's confrontation was gonna be, but I was already praying for strength. I didn't want no problems, just wanted to get settled in my spot and enjoy my night out with the girls and shit. Nothing more, nothing less."

Mikey rolls down the front passenger side window and Meeko turns the music down. "Aye girl, can I get your number?" Mikey jokes causing Mikki to burst out laughing.

"Boy you better stop playing with me and take your little butt to school."

"I'm about to go now Ma. We just dropped Kia off and dad about to take me now."

Meeko gets out the drivers side of the truck and walks around to Mikki's car and leans against the door. "Good Morning." Meeko says sweetly causing Mikki to fight back the urge to melt.

"Can I help you?" She snaps forcing her attitude into the situation

"Just saying good morning is all."

"I think you need to move. Don't think just cause my order aint valid at Inda house that it wont work anywhere else."

"Man shut up. Aint nobody scared of your little ass piece of paper Mikki."

"Well you should be."

"Whatever. So where you headed bright and early this morning?"

"That's not really your business Sir."

"I know your ass aint going to school dressed like that."

"Again, where I'm going or not going for that matter is none of your damn business Meeko the white girl slayer." Mikki laughs at her joke and Meeko finds himself chuckling too.

"That's fucked up Mikki. Here I am trying to be civil to you and…"

"Don't do me no favors sir."

"So really Mikki, where you going with your shit all hanging out?"

"My shit aint hanging out."

"Slim, I saw your pussy print way from the driver seat in the truck Mikki."

"Well stop being a pervert riding around looking at people pussy Meeko."

"That aint people pussy. That's MY Pussy." Meeko tries to touch Mikki's thighs and she slaps his hands away.

"You done lost your fucking mind Meeko."

"I apologize. So look, why you aint going to school today?"

"Because I'm out Meeko. I graduate Monday."

"Congratulations."

"Thanks." Mikki blushes.

"Now I gotta go out and get you a graduation gift. I am invited right?

"Whatever Meeko." Mikki puts the gas nozzle away and attempts to walk away and Meeko grabs her arm and pulls her into a tight hug. "Nigga you better get your hands off me." Mikki says, but never attempts to leave his embrace.

"Can we stop beefing now Mikki?" Meeko asks

sincerely.

"I aint beefing with you Meeko."

"Cool. So can we get rid of all your police ass papers and such now."

"Hell no." Mikki finally pulls out of his embrace and looks him in his eyes so he can know that she is serious. "I don't trust you like that anymore Meeko." She informs him sadly.

"That's fucked up Mikki."

"But it's the truth." An awkward silence settles between the two of them. "Look, I gotta go Meeko."

"Man that bitch ass nigga can wait Mikki. I'm talking to you."

"I gotta go pick up Alana. We have plans."

"Oh Alana big forehead ass getting my pussy now?" Meeko asks towering over Mikki causing their bodies to be pressed together."

"Meeko move. I don't have time to play with you." Mikki whines with her hands on his chest, yet not pushing him away.

Meeko leans in close to her ear and whispers "I'm tryna play with you Mikki. With my tongue." He sticks his hand down the front of her leggings and into her panties to feel her wetness. "That pussy still fat and wet just like I remember. You want me to taste it?" Meeko asks while gently tapping her love button with his middle finger. With her eyes closed and sucking her bottom lip Mikki nods her head yeah just as Mikey blows the truck horn bringing them both out of their trance. Embarrassed, Mikki pulls and away from Meeko.

"I have to go." She states as she rushes to the driver side of her car.

"Aye Mikki, Can I call you later?" Meeko asks then proceeds to suck on the same fingers he had just had buried in her panties.

"Yes. That's fine. Mikki blushes.

"Alright. Meeko blows her a kiss as she gets into her car and drives away.

"I swear I hated Meeko ass. I hated how he still had this fucking hold over me. He had hurt me so bad, yet I couldn't get him off my fucking mind … even before this morning. I hated that after all we had been through, he still knew how to touch my body just right, in a way that melted me to the core. I drove back to Alana's house and had to sit there for some time because his touch had my pussy throbbing and aching for more of him. I swear if Mikey hadn't blown the horn when he did I would came all in that nigga hand. Even though we were on a main street in the middle of morning rush hour with other people at the gas station, I was a finger tap on that pussy away from grinding one out. He knew that shit too. I hated being so weak for him.

After I finally got myself together, I got out the car and went and brought some weed from across the street. By time I finished my transaction Alana was coming out the door. She rolled up while I drove and then once we started putting one in the air I told her about my early morning encounter with my estranged ex. I promise I wanted to fuck Meeko so bad my knees were shaking at this point, and of course her ass was chanting "DO IT! DO IT! DO IT!" from the passenger seat.

We finally made it to my favorite Walmart, a stones throw from Arundel Mills and I did all my odds and ends shopping. Of course, we couldn't be that close to the mall and not hit it up so we did. After a few treats for ourselves, we had lunch and then finally headed back.

I had ignored 3 separate calls from Chico while we were out. I liked him, but he was becoming a true blue bug-a-boo. I had spoke to him the night before and I told him Alana and I was getting some time in today and I would call him later. Yet here he was, determined to interrupt my day. We headed to the grocery store once we got back down to PG County and Chico called again. I wasn't gonna answer but it was clear that if he didn't speak to me her wasn't gonna stop calling. So I did and INSTANTLY got heated. This nigga actually had an attitude and told me he was at my house waiting on me and wanted to know how long it was gonna be before I got there. I had to sit my phone in the shopping cart and walk away to stop the vile and evil shit that was about to escape my mouth. I had told him that we were gonna be getting the house set up right because I wanted shit in order so when I picked the kids up Sunday night they could come straight home. That didn't mean for him to come running his ass over there too. This was our girls day and his ass wasn't needed. I told him I wasn't coming back. I had already handled what I needed to and was spending the night at my mother house. Before he had a chance to protest I hung up on his ass and then started to move through the aisles slower and slower. I was so glad when we got to my house and I didn't see his shit out there cause I would've lost it. I hurried up and put my groceries and shit away and then Alana and I headed back around the way.

I chilled at Alana's house until about 10:30 getting fucked up. We invested in some more smoke and made some incredible hulks and just shot the shit with some of the other girls from around the way. About 10:30, I finally called it a night and got in my car and headed to Oxon Hill. I could've went to my dad's house but two things stopped me. I was drunk, and I didn't care how grown I was, my daddy wasn't going for that shit AT ALL. And I was horny as fuck. I had all intentions of going home, showering and playing with this pussy until I passed out with thoughts of Meeko and our earlier encounter. If he had called like he claimed he wanted to, I would've been ending my night riding his fucking face, but he hadn't called and even though I desperately needed him to make me lay flat on my stomach while he used that dick to dig as deep as humanly possible in me … I was not about to call him. I refused to give him the upper hand in this shit.

Just as I started to think about the way his tougue would feel slowly gliding against my pussy, my phone vibrabted on my thigh and almost sent me into a frenzy. I looked down at my phone and sure enough it was Meeko. I couldn't help but laugh thinking this nigga had some type of ESP connection with my pussy.

I talked to him the rest of my ride home and it was about nothing particular. He asked about my day and I asked about his, and my babies etc. I think we both were working up to where we wanted to go with this. Just as he asked me was I still eating pineapples daily because my pussy was still so sweet, I pulled into my parking lot and shit instantly dried up. Chico was parked in front of my building waiting for me. Steam was legit coming out of my ears as I told Meeko I was gonna call him back. I hung up before he could say anything else and turned my phone off because I was about to put this nigga in his place, and I didn't need him calling back and making shit A bigger problem.

I couldn't even pretend to hide or have control of my attitude when I got out the car. This motherfucka had lost his mind for real but I was damn sure about to help him find it."

Mikki gets out the car and slams her door as Chico

gets out of his. She looks at him in pure disgust. "What are you doing here Chico?"

"What you mean what am I doing here? I think the better question is what are YOU doing here?"

"Excuse me? Last I checked this was my damn house?" Mikki opens the building door and walks in with him following behind her. They walk up to her apartment door and she unlocks and opens the door and they walk in. Chico locks the door as Mikki stands in the dining room looking pissed. Chico turns around and his pissed is matching hers. "Again, I ask, what are you doing here Chico?"

"Is me being here a problem or something Mikki?"

"Yeah it is when you pulling pop ups and shit at MY HOUSE like you crazy and shit."

"Damn, now I gotta be crazy?"

"You must be if you think this shit is okay! Riddle me this Chico, how many times have I popped up on you out the blue at your fucking house?"

"Never. You aint got no reason to. My door is always open to your ass. Fuck I asked you to move in and shit Mikki so come on now you aint making no sense."

"Chico, it's about respect. Respecting a persons time and space are important in a relationship."

"So you feel like I don't respect you Mikki?"

"YOU DON'T!" Mikki yells in his face. "If you did you wouldn't be here right now!"

"I'm still trying to figure out why YOUR ASS is here right now Mikki. Because you told me some shit about spending the night at your mother house tonight."

"And I was going to!" Mikki lies on cue as if it were the actual truth.

"You sure, because when I was kicking it with pops, he told me when y'all talked you said you was at Alana's house chilling and then you were GOING HOME! You aint say shit about going to your damn mother house.

So what's that all about Mikki?"

"Whoa." Mikki looks at him incredulously. "What were you doing with my father Chico?"

"Nothing. Just hanging out. Is that a problem now?" Mikki shakes her head in disbelief and walks away from Chico.

"I went in the bathroom and slammed the door because I needed a minute. I liked Chico, but he was truly tripping and I wasn't on it. What the fuck was he doing with my dad. No man goes and just hangs out with a bitch father just because. We wasn't fucking married. And why was he calling him "Pops". Nigga pet names were not allowed and I was gonna nip this shit immediately with both him and my dad because I didn't appreciate it.

After about 15 minutes, I came out the bathroom and I was completely sober. This shit had blew my high something serious. I walked by Chico sitting in the living room in the dark looking stupid. I went on in the kitchen and made me a big ass turkey and cheese sandwich and then sat at the dinning room table and ate in complete silence. Chico finally turned the TV on. I sat and ate in silence and every so often I would look over at him and catch him looking over at me. Neither of us said it, but this shit was over. It was time to call it a wrap.

After I got finished eating, I went and got in the shower, with the door LOCKED. Since I couldn't fuck Meeko like I was planning too, I got myself off three times back to back with thoughts of him. Once I was done, I got dressed in a full pair of pajamas, I'm talking panties, socks, top and bottoms. Chico was still sitting on the sofa watching TV and I was hoping he got the memo and went the fuck home. Although it was over in my head, I wasn't gonna break up with him tonight … alone… with nobody having my fucking address. While he had been kind and sweet to me since day one, when you break a nigga heart, especially one that was screaming LOVE so easily, they could switch up and I wasn't tryna go through that shit again. Remember Rickey from back in the day? Cause I damn sure remembered him and the ass whooping he gave me when I called myself being done with his shit. I started watching TV and eventually drifted off to sleep.

I don't know what time it was, but Chico eventually came and got in the bed and had the nerve to start playing with my nipples trying to wake me up. He had no clue that he would NEVER feel the inside of these walls again. I pushed the shit out of him, damn near knocking him and his hard dick he had pressed against my ass to the floor. I told him I was on my period and turned back over and went back to sleep.

I woke up the next morning and he was still calling hogs. I got myself together and then woke him up around 9:30 because I had shit to do and he was NOT staying in my shit alone. That's how motherfuckas started moving in and I wasn't on that shit at all. I sat back and ate a bowl of cereal while he took a shower and got dressed in the same shit he had on the day before. Wasn't no leaving no shit behind or nothing and I guess my demeanor let him know this.

Once we both were dressed we left out and he asked about my agenda for the day. I told him I was gonna be busy and would call him later. I really wasn't pushing him off, I did have a busy day ahead. He gave me 1500 dollars and told me to not to forget to pick up my cap and gown today and to get Mikey a really nice birthday gift from him. I knew he was trying to soften me up and a part of me felt bad when he kissed me softly on my cheek and told me he was sorry and that he loved me and hoped I would still let him love me. He was breaking my heart for real. Just him remembering that today was the day I had to pick up my cap and gown and pay my graduation fees meant a lot. While Meeko would've gave me the money to do whatever in the world I needed and wanted to do, he would've never taken the time to remember that I needed to do this by this day because well… it wasn't about him. When I drove off, I felt in a really fucked up space about all this shit. I knew that while Meeko felt good to me, Chico was good for me.

Feeling like the ball of confusion I was, I got on my mission and went and handle my affairs of the day, picking up my graduation stuff and paying all my fees and then stopping at the mall to grab my baby some birthday stuff and a few treats for myself. When I was done, I went to my dad's house because we needed to have a whole conversation about the goings on between him and Chico. I understood that he was cool with him and shit, but I needed him to know I wasn't in this thing as deep as him and Chico so he could stop trying to marry me off to the nigga and giving him insider information. When I got there Betty was home by herself and hit me with a huge surprise. According to her, today was divorce day for Ike and Malissa. They were at court as we spoke and I was speechless. I mean I knew my dad and Betty were engaged and all that shit, but hearing that my parents were getting a real live divorce was still heartbreaking. Despite they had been apart for damn near a decade now.

Betty and I sat around and shot the shit as I went through me and the kids clothes and stuff deciding what to keep and what to donate to the church's upcoming clothing drive. Meeko called while I was there to remind me that Mikey had a PTA meeting that evening at 6pm, and according to him Mikey was insisting that me and him come there together. I knew about the meeting but figured since it was still his time with the kids he would handle it. But he kept insisting that his son was insisting. I eventually agreed to meet them at the school at 6. In true Meeko fashion, he wouldn't leave well enough alone and all but twisted my arm to get me to agree to go and grab something to eat with them afterwards. I agreed to go under the guise of doing this for my babies but truth be told, I missed him like crazy. Even after the way he did me. The heart wanted what the hell the heart wanted even if it was stupid as hell to want it.

After I finished separating the stuff for the clothing drive, I went home to get ready for this evening. I know it was only a PTA meeting and shit, but I felt like I needed to remind him of what he let go of. So I went home, showered, and slipped into a summer dress and heels and pinned my hair up in a bun. My mother called around 4:30 asking if I would meet her and my sisters for dinner tonight because she needed to talk to us but I declined because I had a PTA meeting to attend. Besides, I already knew what she wanted to talk about. Her and my daddy finally being divorced. I wasn't really ready for that conversation so that was another reason I was passing. True I liked Betty and was growing to even love her, I don't think it's a child alive, even when grown that doesn't have that "perfect family" image in their head, and well you can't have that with a big ass divorce chain around your neck. I was sure I would be alright, like I said they had already been apart for damn near 10 years but today I wasn't ready to digest the end of that era.

At 6pm, I was standing in front of Wheatley waiting for the them when they pulled up. When they got out the car I found myself subconsciously licking my lips while watching them walk towards me. Meeko was looking good enough to eat ... or suck. I could tell he had done just as I did, pulled out the stops to show me what I had been missing out on. His line up was FRESH and CRISP as a motherfucka and everything he had on had a newness about it. I wanted to control the smile that was spread across my face as they approached but I couldn't. I had a beautiful ass family.

When they walked up to me, Mikey hugged me first and Mykia damn near jumped into my arms. I missed them so much. Without warning, Meeko hugged me and kissed me on my cheek and I swear fire shot through my whole body. I had to take a step back to regain my composure. We went in and met with Mikey teacher and she was singing his little ass praises. For the most part he was a good kid and smart as a whip. He had his moments, but I already knew that. He was my child and his father's blood ran through him so yeah there were days I knew she wished his ass had stayed home from school. All in all his report was great and he was at the top of his class. She wanted to recommend him skipping 4th grade and going straight on to 5th. Meeko was all for it but I wasn't because even though he was performing at a 5th grade level Mikey ass was immature as hell and I wanted more time to think about it. I was so proud of him. Even if Meeko and I couldn't get our shit together, we had definitely done something right when it came to our kids.

We left Mikey's class beaming with pride at the job our son was doing. True he transferred in the middle of the year but it proved to be the best thing for him as they were seeing his full potential on most days when he wasn't being truly his father's child. We were heading for the exit discussing where we were gonna have dinner when I heard my name being called from behind. It was a child's voice so I had no clue who it would be. I turned around just in time to see Chico's daughter Aaliyah breaking away from the lady she was with and running at me full speed. She ran up to me and hugged me so tight I had to pass Mykia back to Meeko to keep her damn legs from getting crushed."

"Mikki! I missed you!" Aaliyah beams with excitement as she continues to hug Mikki.

"Hey Aaliyah. You look so cute. I love your hair like this."

"Thank you. My auntie did it for me. You wanna see my report card? I got two A's, two B's and the rest C's. Are you proud of me?"

"Of course. You a smart little cookie huh."

"Yes." Aaliyah blushes, still holding on to Mikki.

The three women Aaliyah is with walk up to Mikki, Meeko and the kids. "What's up Meeko." Lanay states while grilling Mikki.

"Aint shit."

"Where your fuck ass cousin at?"

"Lanay beat it for real. My kids right here. Watch your mouth."

"My bad. But you need to tell him to step up. Same way you at your son PTA meeting he should've been here for his."

"Slim that's between y'all."

"Come on Aaliyah, You all running up to strangers and shit." Sandy says while eyeing Mikki with Malice.

"She not no stranger aunt Sandy. This my daddy girlfriend Mikki. I know her!" Aaliyah snaps at her mother's sister with an attitude.

" I'm your dad's friend Aaliyah." Mikki quickly corrects as she takes in the incredulous looks everyone is giving her including Meeko.

"Well he said you are his girlfriend." Aaliyah counters in confusion.

"I'm a girl and I'm his friend. Nothing more. Nothing less." Mikki says with finality.

"Oh. Okay." Aaliyah says sadly.

"You keep up the good work in school okay." Mikki pats her on her back and takes Mykia back and they start to walk away.

"A part of me felt like shit for denying my relationship with Chico but it caught me off guard. I hadn't told Meeko I was dating anyone else and apparently Mikey hadn't either and I appreciated that. The look on his face when her little ass called me her daddy girlfriend is what caused the lies to come tumbling out of my mouth. It was somewhere between surprise disbelief and hurt. And knowing that something made him feel that way made me want to do whatever I had to do to fix it... including lie and deny my relationship with Chico.

Meeko was quiet until we got outside and I braced myself for what he had to say about what he had just heard. Although he hurt me with his antics, what he though and felt about who I was keeping time with mattered to me. Partially because the only person I wanted to be keeping time with was him and we all know men are wired different. Whereas a woman could let go of the fact that a dude messed around with somebody she knew, a dude would hold that shit to heart. All a man would be able to see is the fact that this other man knows what her fuck face looks like and that ego wouldn't let him look beyond that.

True I had been with other guys in the time Meeko and I rode this merry-go-round but Rickey was on the other side of the city and Raji was dead so Meeko never had to deal with other people knowing somebody else had been in his home. This was different and I was truly scared that him hearing this would unravel whatever little progress we made and stop whatever was getting ready to happen before it even got started.

Once we got outside he asked me to ride with them to Carmine's where we were having dinner. I agreed and parked my car down the street at my dad's house. The ride downtown was awkward. Like nobody said anything, not even the kids. I couldn't even use the time to get my own thoughts together because I couldn't stop worrying about exactly what Meeko and Mikey were thinking. We found parking and walked to the restaurant and were seated very quickly. I was about to regret even coming because I couldn't do the next two hours or so sitting in this uncomfortable silence we all had seemed to settle into.

Finally, After we order our drinks and received them, Meeko broke the silence by imitating our overly perky waitress and it got us to laughing, which lead to us talking and the awkwardness of the evening was gone. We sat as a family and ate good, laughed hard and enjoyed each others company. I really missed this. I really missed us. Not just Meeko and I, but us as a family.

When we were done, we drove up by Union Station and parked and took a stroll through Lower Senate Park. I loved this park at night when the fountains would light up. While Mikey busied himself chasing his sister around, Meeko and I sat on a bench and finally he broke his silence about the secret he was let in on thanks to a big mouthed ass child."

"Of all the niggas in the world Mikki?" Meeko asks while shaking his head in disbelief.

"Don't start Meeko. Besides, he and I are just friends."

"But why?"

"But why what? Why did I move on? Because you left me. You chose the white girl over what we shared and that hurt Meeko."

"Well to be clear YOU actually left me. And I wasn't asking why you moved on, just why you moved on with this nobody ass nigga. That's what I'm not able to understand."

"Chico is a sweet guy Meeko."

"That's my point." Meeko laughs. "Mikki he soft as shit. A straight pussy. If you was out to start fucking with niggas I know and shit, why you aint go after Hank or Stevie or one of them niggas. Niggas I know can provide for you and protect you when I aint around nomore.

"Well first of all, again, Chico and I are just friends

Meeko."

"Y'all gotta be more than that with his peoples all claiming you and shit."

"And furthermore, you do not get to pick who I move on, or build friendships with. And incase you didn't know it, I don't need nobody to to take of me nigga. That's why I have an education and a bomb ass CAREER, not job but CAREER that I jump into July 6th and…."

"I get all that, but every woman needs a man she can lean on when shit get tough. Be it a hard day at the office or a nigga in traffic got you fucked up. Everybody need somebody they can turn to. And I'm sorry but that nigga Chico a straight gump. He done let niggas rob him off and be out on the block within the hour selling his shit and he aint do nothing. He a pussy and you don't need that. Shit, you and your sisters go harder than this bitch ass nigga."

Mikki laughs at Meeko statement for a few seconds and then gets serious. "While all that may be true Meeko, the most important thing for me after being with you is having somebody in my life who first and foremost respects me as a whole. Having someone who treats me right and handles with the love and care I deserve. Chico does that. I don't have to worry about him hitting on me, or choking me, or cheating on me or…."

"Okay I get it!" Meeko snaps to cut her off, hating where she is going with their conversation. "Listen Mikki, I know I fucked up big time with you …."

"REPEATEDLY." Mikki interrupts.

"You right. Repeatedly. And I know you probably don't believe shit I'm about to say but Mikki I love you. I love you and I'm still IN love with you. But I know I did you wrong and now you getting your life on. So I'ma give you space to do that, but I need you to know I'm not giving up on us. You gonna be my wife one day … soon."

"Is that right?"

"Mark my words. But in the mean time, I'ma put the ball in your court and let you have your moment in the sun. But soon and very soon, I'm coming for what's mine." Meeko leans in and kisses Mikki softly on the lips and then gets up to go and chase Mykia with Mikey.

"While his kiss was soft and sweet, it was enough to send my body into overdrive. I sat there on the bench squeezing my legs together trying to calm that heartbeat between my legs because I wanted him soooooo fucking bad. I finally joined him in playing with the kids for awhile and then we saw a rat and broke out. Mikey and Mykia were sleep before we got of the parking space good, so Meeko and I ended up riding in silence. Each lost in our own thoughts.

We pulled up in front of my dad's house and both just sat there. I didn't want to leave and he didn't want me to leave but I guess both of us were too stubborn to give in."

"Before I forget, are we giving this dude the skating rink party he keep asking for?" Meeko asks, glad to have a conversation that will keep Mikki in his presence awhile longer.

"Yeah that's cool. I will go over there tomorrow and set it all up."

"What time you gonna go?"

"Probably about 12. I'm planning to sleep in. Enjoy these few days of peace and quiet before the kids come home." Mikki smiles thinking about having her babies back at home.

"How much you think you gonna need to cover it all, cause I can run it over here when I drop them off in the morning. Or I can give you my card now cause I don't have no cash on me." Meeko lies.

"I think I can cover it this go round."

"Look, I'm paying for this so chill. As a matter of fact, you wanna follow me out to the house to get it tonight?" Meeko asks hoping Mikki picks up on the double entendre.

Mikki blushes having caught it immediately. "Wont the white girl be there?"

"Despite what you think, shorty is not my woman and she don't stay with me. I live alone two weeks out of the month now."

"I'll just get it from you tomorrow."

"What time you gonna come out to the house?"

"I'll be there around 10."

"That's cool. That will give me time to drop them off, check on Janiya and then get back home."

"How is she doing?"

"She good. Growing up fast." Meeko shakes his head hating the influences his daughter has in her life because of her mother.

"Alright then, I will see you at 10 Sir."

"Cool. Oh and leave your panties at home." Meeko says seductively while biting his bottom lip.

"Whatever." Mikki blushes and then gets out the truck.

"I walked to the house blushing the whole way while Meeko sat in the truck and watched me

to make sure I got in okay. I waved bye to him before closing the door. I had decided I didn't feel like driving all the way out to my place so I was crashing here.

I went upstairs and saw that my daddy and Betty were both asleep, so I went in my room and stripped down to nothing and just laid in the bed thinking. I hated this game Meeko and I were playing. I loved this nigga with all my heart and just wanted to be with him forever. I knew on some level he loved me also, but why couldn't he just do right by me? Like why couldn't every day of our relationship be like today. All smiles, all laughs and all love. Why did shit have to constantly be complicated with him? I didn't have the answers to any of these questions and I'm positive he didn't have them either. I closed my eyes and said a silent prayer for Meeko and I. I just prayed that God would lead us in the right direction and help us overcome all the foolishness and drama. Even if it wasn't meant for us to be together, we had to children we would spend forever being Mommy and Daddy to, so I wanted us to at least be able to get to a point that we could do that without the bullshit.

After I said my prayers, I closed my eyes and started to drift off to sleep. I figured the faster I went to sleep the quicker morning would come and I could go and "get that" from Meeko.

The next morning, I was up at 6am even though I hadn't planned to be up that early. The commotion from downstairs got me up. I found a pair of sweats and a t shirt and threw it on and headed downstairs. I heard my daddy's voice but didn't know who the hell he was talking to until I reached the bottom of the stairs. I immediately started screaming and jumped in their arms. MY SISTERS WERE HOME!

Amber and her Man Travis were here with their set of adorable twin boys Travell and Tyrell. While Amber had told us all about Travis and while she was pregnant we talked all the damn time, but we had yet to meet him and the boys. Amber had left New York some time ago and headed to LA with the dream of being an actress. My daddy was dead set against that shit and swore Amber had lost her mind. While she didn't find her dream career, she did find the man of her dreams in Travis. Travis was an R&B Superstar if you will and he was smitten with Amber from the day they met in Starbucks. In no time flat she moved to San Diego with him and then the twins came about a year later. When I went to LA with Nikki, I wanted to go and see her and her family, but they were in the London at the time as Travis was on tour and he was adamant about having his family with him at all times. They had been back in the States a whole two weeks and decided to come here so we could meet them, and she could be here for my graduation. I was in tears hugging my sisters because I was so happy we all would be together again even if just for a little while.

Betty made breakfast and we all sat and ate and played catch up. I could see the pride in my daddy's eyes sitting at the table with his soon to be new bride, three of his five daughters, two of his three son-in-laws and two of his five grandchildren. I sat around with them until about 8:30 and then I went to go take a shower and get dressed because although I was excited to see my family, I had things to do. I would have more than enough time to spend with them as they were gonna be in town until July 7th. So, we definitely had time to hang!

After I got dressed and told them I would be back shortly, and we were gonna go get our mother and go to lunch and such I was in the wind headed to Laurel. I put on a strapless summer dress with no bra or panties on under it because cutting the bullshit, Meeko and I both knew what I was driving all the way out Laurel for and it wasn't no damn money for no damn skate party. Mikey school was a block from my dad's house. Meeko could've dropped that money off when he took him to school, but he wanted to fuck and well, I wanted to get fuck so off to

Laurel I went.

We ended up meeting each other at the light, so I followed him to the house and parked behind him in the driveway. I sat and watched him as he got out and he looked so fucking good in a pair of Khaki shorts, fresh New Balance and a white t shirt. He made even the simplest shit look so good, and I swear my pussy got wetter at the sight of his ass. I damn near came from pure anticipation. He went to the back of the truck and was getting some grocery bags out, I got out and helped him by closing the rear lift door and grabbing his keys to open the house door. When we got to the doorway, He pressed his body against mine making sure I felt how hard he was. I damn near broke the key off trying to get that motherfucka in the door because I couldn't wait another minute. Apparently neither could he.

He closed the door and dropped the bags right where they were and pulled me to him and stuck his tongue down my throat. Without an ounce of resistance, I threw my arms around his neck and hopped up on him wrapping my legs around his waist. The friction from my bare pussy rubbing up against him alone was about to send me into orbit as he cupped my ass that was completely exposed and started to grind me against the swollen bulge in his shorts. With my lips pressed against his, in a damn near begging tone I asked him to fuck me please and without a word he obliged. Meeko turned us around and my back was against the door as he freed his dick from his pants and placed it against my opening. I held on for dear life as he pushed into me with so much force I couldn't help but cry out at the mix of pleasure and pain. As if that wasn't enough, He held me in place being sure that neither of us moved a muscle and I felt every single solid inch of him as my pussy contracted around his love muscle, soaking it with my juices. My body was on fire as he started to move again and slowly grinded his dick against my walls deep inside of me. I couldn't control the tears coming from my eyes as I called out to him letting him know I loved him as my body gave way, and clutched him tight as I came so hard it left me lightheaded. I held onto him gasping, trying to catch my breath and regain my composure as he lowered me and my feet hit the floor. I was putty in his hands as he told me to take my ass upstairs and wait for him because I had been a bad girl and was gonna pay for that shit. He smacked my ass so hard it stung but it felt so good. I couldn't say a word as I made my way up the stairs on baby giraffe legs. I didn't know what Meeko had instore for me, but I was ready, willing and able to take it all … and I did … Literally.

There wasn't an inch of my body Meeko didn't taste or a hole he didn't plug. There were monkey bites, ass slaps, deep scratches and tears all tied up in the mix of our love making. When we were finally done, and my body had nothing else left to give, Meeko and I both passed out. We both slept sticky and in the wet spot with no complaints. When we finally woke up, it was a little after 5pm. I grabbed my phone and saw I had calls and messages galore. Mikey had gone to my dad's house after school when Meeko didn't show up and everybody else who called were just trying to find out where I was. Understandable considering I had my sisters waiting on me and all. Chico had called a few times and left messages letting me know he needed to speak to me ASAP. I wasn't thinking about no damn Chico. I already knew them bitches went back and told him that I denied our relationship, but I didn't care. The shit was already over in my head and me fucking Meeko had just sealed the deal for me.

Meeko and I both sat in the bed returning text messages to let people know we were alright because a whole fucking day had gotten away from us. Since Mykia had to be picked up by 6 and it was already 5:15, Meeko asked Inda to go pick her up. At first, she texted him back hell no, so he pulled me next to him and snapped a picture of us together in the bed looking like we had been to war and sent it to her. Her ass texted back QUICK "OKAY!!! Love yall". While we both sat and laughed at Inda's craziness, him sending that picture scared me. It scared me because it made me think about the true state of our relationship. I loved Meeko and I wanted us to get back together, grow together and get married and live the rest of our days happy as husband and wife. My heart longed for that, but I didn't know where Meeko stood. I know what he said, shit, he had been saying it for damn near 10 years now, BUT the fact of the matter was his actions were ALWAYS the polar opposite. For all I knew today could've been just about fucking me one more time for him. Or his way to get me to drop those orders. I didn't know. And now that people knew I was over here letting him buss it wide open... because Inda ass couldn't hold water ... I felt some kind of way in my heart. I just didn't want to end up looking stupid once again. Especially considering I had just thrown away a relationship with an amazing dude, who although it was early in our shit, he wanted the same things I wanted.

I finally pulled myself from the comforts of the bed because it was time to find out where we really stood."

"Can you give me a wash cloth and towel please." Mikki asks.

Meeko slides over to the side of the bed she is

standing on and pulls her back into his arms. "For what? We aint done yet."

"Is that right?" Mikki blushes. "I think I'ma have to take a rain check. My sisters are waiting on me and…"

"Aint nobody thinking about no Vikki."

Mikki laughs. "Boy hush. But Nikki and Amber are here and we all were supposed to have lunch and shit. Now I guess it will be dinner. Yooo, I almost forgot. You will never guess who Amber is married to."

"Her fat ass got married?" Meeko jokes.

Mikki pops his hand playfully. "Ole girl done came down a lot. But she is MARRIED to Travis Morris Meeko. I was stuck on stupid this morning seeing his ass sitting across the table from me at breakfast."

"Get the fuck outta here. Thee Travis Morris, Mr. Baby Come home with T married Fats?

"You so wrong Meeko." Mikki laughs. "But yeah, they met, fell in love, had twins and eloped."

"Damn why all your sisters stay eloping? Probably because of y'all goofy ass father."

"Hell if I know. All I know is when it's my time, wont be no lonely hilltop or court building. I'm doing it big."

"Is that right? So who you marrying Mikki? Chico?"

"Boy Bye!" Mikki smooches his face. "You play too much but one of these days, somebody is gonna come along and fall head over heels for ole girl and damn near break their ankles getting my ass down the aisle."

"Is that right?" Meeko asks, looking deep in Mikki's eyes.

"It is."

"So that's what you really want Mikki? You want to be married?"

Mikki sists down beside Meeko. "I want something real Meeko. I want to be loved, respected, protected, cherished. And yes I do want to have somebody to spend my forever with."

"Just somebody or…"

"Cut the shit Meeko. You know I want you. Always have. Even when you have hurt me to my core. I still love and want you. I just don't want to keep being hurt in order to have you.

"I can dig it. Look, not to change the subject but can you do me a favor?"

"What's that? Stay here while I go and pick up the kids."

"Meeko I told you my sisters…"

Meeko stands up and kisses Mikki passionately leaving her breathless. "You told me what you want, and you got that Mikki. Now I need the time to tell you what I want so we can better understand each other and move forward together."

"Is that right?" Mikki blushes.

"Very much so. Now go ahead and take a bath and chill. I'mma go grab them and some pizza and shit and come back and we gonna fix this… fix us. You with me?"

"You know I am." Mikki stands on her tippy toes and kisses Meeko.

"And I'm sure by time I get back you will have called your folks and let him know it's a wrap." Meeko smacks Mikki on the ass and then walks into the bathroom in his bedroom and turns on the shower.

"I didn't say another word, just went and joined him in the shower. Without warning, I dropped to my knees and took him to another world. I just wanted to please him so I did. Once we finished showering, I managed to find a

romper of mine at the back of my old closet and threw it on. I pinned my hair up in a bun and rode with him to get the kids. We picked up Mykia first and Inda was damn near in tears when we came through the door together. She was soooo dramatic. After we got Mykia, we were headed to my dad's house but came up on Mikey and his friends walking from the store. My sisters were pissed that I stood them up and I really didn't need the world seeing me with Meeko until we talked and got to the bottom of us or fixed us as he said. So, we told him to go get his backpack and stuff and just let them know that Meeko was outside and not to mention that I was too. Mikey was just so happy to see both of his parents he aint care about nothing else. He said he would get his backpack later and hopped in the truck and we left. I called the house and let Betty know that I had Mikey and would get his stuff later so nobody wouldn't be worried about him. We went and got Fish from Horace and Dickies down H Street and picked up ice cream and went back to Meeko's. We watched a movie with the kids while we ate and then played Uno with Mikey while we all also had to participate in a tea party with Mykia.

Once the kids went to bed, Meeko and I were back at it again. I missed how good this man felt inside of me. I missed the smell of his body laying next to mine. I missed the sound of his breathing at night. I missed him. When we finally called it a night, I just laid in his arms and neither of us said a thing for awhile. Then with his face laying on the side of mine, he simply said "I'm gonna show you Mikki. No more talk. All action. Just wait and see."

Now Meeko had promised me changes before when it came to his bullshit, so a person with good sense would've taken it with a grain of salt. However, I was his certified fool so I took it to heart. That and the fact that it felt different this time. Like maybe us REALLY being a part was the wake up he needed. I laid in his arms and cried myself to sleep. For once, not in pain. But surrounded in joy. I had my family back together and I knew this time we had to win.

I was certain of it.

I got up the next morning and made breakfast for my family while they were asleep. They woke up to Pancakes, eggs, turkey bacon, and fresh fruit. We sat at the table and had breakfast while finalizing things for Mikey's birthday party that was a week away. Once we were done, we started to get dressed because I had some shopping to do and I needed to go make it up to my sisters for my disappearing act I pulled. I also planned to go grab a few things from my spot while I was out. Once we were all put together, Meeko took my car and I took the Escalade, him and Mikey went off in one direction and Mykia and I went off in another. My first stop was gonna be my apartment because I had on a pair of leggings, no bra or panties and T shirt. So I needed to get dressed but while I was talking to my sisters on the drive over, they were like BITCH COME GET US because they knew my ass could get lost quick and wasn't going for being stood up today. Vikki was already at my dad's house and Michelle had church business so we would see her at dinner the following day. I stopped at my dad's and grabbed Nikki, Vikki and Amber and we headed out to my apartment with them giving me hell all the way about how I ditched them and how Michelle was so upset that I wasted her time blah blah blah. Fuck her.

As we drove closer to my building, I was glad I didn't go home alone, because guess who was parked there sitting and waiting. You right. Mr. Chico ass. I started to buck a U and just buy something from the damn mall, thinking he didn't recognize me because I wasn't driving my car. I completely forgot how long this Escalade was mine, so he knew it too because as soon as he saw it coming down he got out his truck. He looked like shit. Like a total madman and for the first time I was afraid of this man that had been so docile and loving towards me. The look in his eyes just screamed "Bitch I'ma kill you!" and fuck what you heard, I wasn't trying to die. I promise I wasn't gonna get out, but you know Vikki and Nikki hadn't changed so they both hopped out the truck first ready for whatever. I was praying this nigga aint have no gun on him and come here on some everybody dies shit. I had my daughter with me, and her or my sisters didn't deserve to be caught up in my shit.

As soon as we got out I gave Amber my keys and told her which apartment was mine so she could get my baby out of harm's way. I had to face the music for how I had done Chico. It was time."

"What's up Chico? You good bro?" Nikki asks, looking like she's ready to pounce on him at any moment.

"Yeah I'm good. Just waiting to speak to your lying ass sister"

"Well damn, good morning to you too Chico." Mikki tries to make light of the situation.

"I'm sure it is a good morning for you, considering your ass aint come the fuck home last night!"

"Aye Chico, I think you need to chill out slim." Vikki interrupts. "I understand you might be feeling some type of way about shit, but you can't be speaking to my sister like that."

"Its okay Vikki, I got this. Y'all go ahead in the house."

"Nah, we'll wait on the porch." Nikki grabs Vikki by the arm and pulls her over to the porch of Mikki's building and they sit down.

Mikki turns back to Chico. "Well you know they aint gonna go nowhere. So what's up?"

"You tell me Mikki?" I'm hearing from other motherfuckas about how they saw my girl out playing the happy family role and shit down at the school… How… get this shit … my girl broke it down to my child how I aint shit but her friend in front of everybody… then left with her baby daddy and shit. Then I'm calling and calling and calling your ass and you can't even pick up the fucking phone and say boo! Then yesterday, my mother on her way down H Street and guess who she told me she seen in the truck with another nigga … none other than your busy body ass! It aint take long to figure out who you were with since her dumb ass couldn't give an accurate description of the truck. All it took was for me to roll up on Mikey homeboys and ask where he was and they all like "his father came and got him." I gave them each 10 dollars and then asked if you were in the truck with him and they were like yeah."

"Wow." Mikki says in disbelief. "So you in other words have lost your motherfucking mind running up on my sons friends asking them ANY motherfucking thing about me! About him! Or about Meeko!"

"Why you gotta try and play a nigga Mikki! I love your motherfucking ass!"

"No nigga you love the IDEA of me! You barely even know me, how the fuck could you possibly love me!"

"Oh but I guess you believe that Meeko bitch ass does huh? This nigga done fucked you over so many times and you keep on running right the fuck back to him! What the fuck is you retarded Mikki!"

"Are you done Chico? Cause all the shit you saying is moot. We done."

"So you just gonna go right back to another bad decision."

"If that's what you wanna call it, fine. But the bottom line is we are done."

"You sad as shit Mikki. I always thought you was so smart, and so beautiful but I see you just like every other trash ass bitch around here. See my problem was I cared about your ass, I treated you right and that aint what y'all hoes want. Now if I fucked every bitch that breathed right in your face, or put my hands on your ass you would be leaping tall buildings in a single bound trying to be with a nigga."

"You really standing here wasting your whole breath Chico."

"Nah, I'm done with it. You win. But in a few weeks, when that AIDS case waiting to happen get caught with his dick rammed up in somebody else AGAIN, and your poor little heart is all broken and crushed, bitch don't call me. Accept your fate of a life long subscription of penicillin pills and new baby mommas and stay the fuck away from me." Chico gets in his truck and slams the door. He starts it up and backs out the space and speeds off.

"I stood there in shock for the longest time like yoooooo I know this nigga aint just read me the riot act and then peel out leaving his whole tire marks on the ground? I didn't want to hurt Chico, but shit happened. Besides, like I had said I was ready for this shit to be over with anyway, so I was glad he did it.

I spent the day hanging out with my sisters and after they all gave me the blues for jumping down the rabbit hole once again, we ended up having a really good girl's day out. We rode up to Baltimore and had crabs and drinks, did some light shopping and just enjoyed each other's company. I hadn't realized how much I missed having my sisters around until I had them around again. Like even though Vikki was still here in DC, she had her own life as well so we didn't get together as much as we should have. But we were all together now and I was loving it.

On Sunday morning, I was up early and headed to the city for church with my family. My dad was so excited to have all his girls and grandkids and son-in-laws in the building. I asked Meeko to come, even tried to bribe him by making him CUM but still no haps. I didn't complain or throw a fit because well, Meeko had never been into going to church with us so I wasn't surprised when he said no. I just thought it would be nice to have my man there with me also. He did agree to go to dinner with us at Michelle's that evening, so I took the consolation prize and me and the kids bopped on to the city for a morning of praise and worship with my family. Both blood and spiritual.

My daddy, as usual, was showing out in the pulpit that morning. I don't know if it was the energy of being surrounded by his family so heavily or what, but Ike was channeling his inner TD Jakes that morning. I was LOVING IT! While I may have been a heathen in a lot of people's eyes, my relationship with God and respect of his word was 100% pure. I felt all kinds of blessed this morning. Meeko and I were working things out. I was starting a new journey in my life. I was surrounded by those I loved and those who loved me. Yeah, I was truly feeling the blessings until it was time for tithes and offerings and guess who stalker ass was in the building. None other than Chico himself. He came through the tithing line praising God's name like he wasn't sitting up in there being blasphemes as hell. He was there simply because of me. He looked at me and smiled as he passed me by and it took everything in me not to spit in his fucking face. My daddy caught the looks me and my sisters were holding as he came by, then I remembered I hadn't actually shared with my daddy that Chico and I were done. Shit, as much as he had been burying his head up my father ass lately I was surprised HE hadn't called him crying and shit and told him. He was good for shit like that. Which was one of the main reasons it was hard for me to take him seriously... aside from just moving way too fucking fast for my liking.

I had to force myself to stay in the moment of praise and worship and not focus on the fact that the DEVIL was here in the flesh trying his damn best to steal my joy! Once service was over I headed outside to address him and his bullshit immediately. I stood outside waiting and waiting but he NEVER came out. I finally went back in and he was gone. He went out the back door like the bitch he was. I went back outside and called him and left him a message letting him know this was his one and only warning to stay the fuck away from me and my family or I promised to God I was gonna let that monster named Meeko loose on his ass and we both knew that wasn't what he wanted. I was praying Chico took heed to my warning because I really didn't want Meeko to get involved, BUT if he kept up his Michelle N Dechello act, he would leave me no choice.

Later that evening, I ended up skipping dinner with my family. I went home ... meaning Meeko's house ... to change and make the mac and cheese I was supposed to bring when my dad called me raising hell about Chico. Apparently, he called my dad and told him I was running around behind his back with Meeko. My daddy called himself lecturing me when I told him yes Meeko and I were very much back together. He started going in but I had to pump his breaks and remind him of a few things... I'm grown and this is my relationship. Chico was a great fit for HIM, but my heart is where it wants to be and that's that. I told my daddy I loved him and was gonna go ahead and end the call now because I didn't want to be disrespectful, BUT he was way over his boundaries. While I missed out on the togetherness of dinner with my siblings and parents, because even my mom was there, I was okay because I was at home with the family that meant the world to me,

I was up super early the next morning because it was my graduation day and I couldn't wait! I had worked so hard for this day and it was finally here. I was out early getting my hair and nails done and by 5pm I was finally walking across the stage with my degree. My family both blood and extended was there, including Alana and Eric, Inda, Gerald, Santana and the whole gang. When they called my name the hooting and whistling from my own little cheering section had me overwhelmed. I remember back when I was 14 and pregnant with Mikey, nobody thought this day would come for me. Truthfully speaking not even me. I was young, scared, and even though I had a huge support system a part of me thought I'd never do more or be more than a Baby Mother. I wanted more, knew I deserved more but thought having a child so young would limit me. It took some time, but I finally realized the only limitations I have in my life are the ones I put on myself. Now here I was.

After the graduation, we all went to dinner and it was amazing. Inda had closed down the whole restaurant in my honor so we could have a family celebration. We took so many pictures, and downed so many glasses of wine in between enjoying a seafood spread that was out of this world. Halfway through the shindig I got nervous because I looked over and saw Meeko and my daddy in a conversation that looked intense. Just the two of them off in a corner. Being that they didn't talk to each other at all, I was scared all hell was about to break loose. I just knew my daddy was over there suggesting that Meeko sit down and let Chico and I have a chance at love. I decided I was gonna just kill Ike and get the shit over with because he was so into this fucking dude and I wanted nothing to do with him at this point. And I was not about to sit by idle and let him fuck up my family trying to single handedly save a ship that had already sunk. I got up from where I was sitting and was headed in their direction when my mother came out of nowhere and linked her arm in mine and walked me back in the opposite direction talking about let's take a picture. If some shit broke out between Meeko and my daddy and they got to throwing blows I was gonna kill her ass.

After a shitload of pictures, it was time to finally sit down and open my gifts. I was soooooo excited because what girl didn't love gifts! I had a huge table full of stuff and I couldn't wait to dive into the shit. My dad and Meeko finally came from being tucked in their corner to join us for the gift opening. Once every gift was opened my daddy went into his suit inside pocket and pulled out and envelope and handed it to my mother. With a smile as big as sunshine I opened it and it was a beautiful card from them. It had been years since I had a card signed by both of them. That alone had me misty eyed but then when I actually read the check that was in there the tears started falling heavy. It was a check for 75,000 made out to me from me and the memo lined said "Follow Your Dreams Babygirl". I collapsed into my parents with real tears falling. Once I got myself together I tried to give it back to them. I mean it was generous as hell, but my parents weren't rich by far. Comfortable... yes. Rich ... Hell NAH! Not hand your kid of 75 stacks rich anyway. I didn't know if they had mortgaged the house or some shit to be able to give me such a lavish gift. My mother took the lead in telling me to take the money, stop being dramatic and go and do whatever it was I wanted to do in this world. Start my own design company or something. Whatever made me smile, just go and do it. My daddy finished it up by telling me he started college funds for each of us when we were born. This was the proceeds of mine since Meeko and I paid for my education. The money was mine and they wanted me to have it. I hugged them both and cried some more, thinking this would be the highlight of my evening....

Then I turned around and Meeko was behind me on one knee. I literally thought I was gonna pass

*out. Like it took me a minute to gather that
everybody had gotten so quiet and he was here ...
in the moment ... on his knee ... the tears started
before he even opened his mouth, once he spoke,
there wasn't a dry eye in the building.*

"Marissa, I know I haven't always shown you. But
you've always meant so much to me. You've been by my
side through so much. On most days, I didn't deserve you
but you still for some reason kept finding the strength to
love someone like me. Someone who is selfish most days,
inconsiderate .... Spiteful. Those are just some of the things
you shared with me overtime about myself. That's the clean
version y'all." Meeko jokes to calm his own nerves
causing the whole room to laugh with him and Mikki. "But
Mikki, I promise you. If you will have me, I will spend
every day for the rest of my life making up for all the tears
I put in your eyes." Meeko turns to look at Ike who has his
own tears in his eyes. "Mr. Washington, would you do me
the honor of giving me your daughter hand in marriage?"
Every eye in the room focuses on Ike waiting for him to
spazz out knowing how he feels about Meeko. Surprisingly
to everyone, Ike smiles warmly and nods at Meeko.
"Anything to see my baby girl happy. You have my
blessing son."
        Everybody in the room starts cheering as Mikki
drops to her knees and throws her arms around Meeko
screaming yes repeatedly before he even has a chance to
officially ask her. Meeko stands up and pulls her up and
pulls out a ring box and opens it causing everyone to gasp
in awe at the amazing 2.5 karat black and white diamond
engagement ring. With shaking hands, Meeko pulls the ring
from the box and slides it on Mikki's finger then looks at

her with eyes full of love. "Mikki, will you do me the honor of being my wife?"

"Yes Meeko, Yes I will!"

Meeko wraps his arms around her waist and pulls her in for another kiss and the entire room erupts with cheers and whistles of congratulations for the newly officially engaged couple.

"I promise I felt like I was floating on a whole cloud the remainder of the night. Everybody congratulated us at some point or another in the night. The most memorable moment for me aside from the proposal was being in the middle of the floor, slow dancing with my husband to be with my head against his chest just listening to his heart beat. Just like the very first time Meeko and I danced together all those years ago back at Nakita's house party, SWV's weak came on and everyone else in the world disappeared. It was just Meeko and I… Together forever, forever together. I was FINALLY gonna be this man wife….

Or so I thought.

****

Keep your eyes peeled for

Mikki And Meeko 3: At Last

Coming Soon!

Check out these other SODCP titles coming soon!

Queen of DC 4: The Book of Revelations
By K Sherrie
(Revised with Alternate Ending)

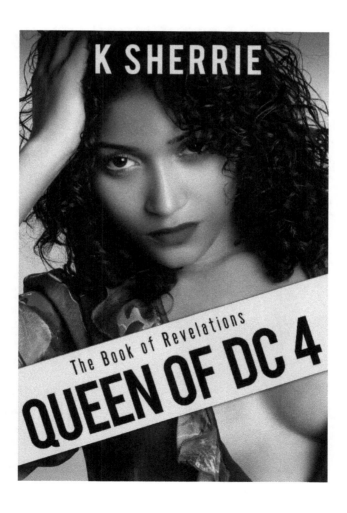

In Love with The Queen of DC : Juan's Story
By K Sherrie

Bestie: Tales of a Twisted Heart
By K Sherrie

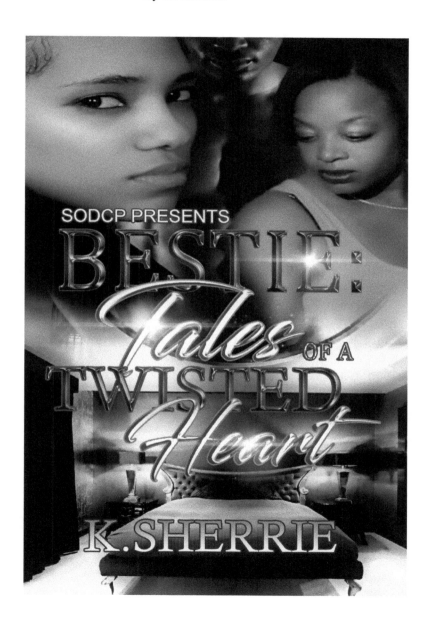

Stay social with K Sherrie on

Facebook @
https://www.facebook.com/iamksherrie4life

Twitter @Ksherrie2014

Instagram @iamksherrie

K Sherrie's Official Website @
www.ksherrie2014.webs.com

As always, reviews are respected and appreciated. Thank you tremendously for your continued support.

K Sherrie

CPSIA information can be obtained
at www.ICGtesting.com
Printed in the USA
LVHW110822241121
704247LV00012BA/1348